1

A NIGHTTIME ESCAPADE

"IT'S RIGHT OVER HERE. C'MON, HURRY UP BEFORE THEY see us," Taylor Harris said as he gripped a tall tree and beckoned to the young woman behind him. "Seriously, stop being such a wuss, Carol. Just grab my hand and follow me. Please. *Pretty please.*"

Taylor gazed at Carol Chambers with a set of big, wet puppy eyes and a pouting lip. He was begging for her company.

Like a shy child, Carol clasped her hands behind her back, twirled her foot in the mud, and glanced around. To her left, campers and counselors of all shapes and sizes marched down the dirt path and headed to a campfire. To her right, she could see a row of cabins. A few lights lit up the log buildings, but only the moon and stars illuminated the woods. It was a beautiful night—a *romantic* night.

And Carol was a sucker for beautiful, romantic nights.

She was a senior counselor at Camp Blaze. So, she was dressed like the other counselors at the camp—a mint green button-up shirt, dark green shorts, brown boots. Her curly black hair bounced on her shoulders with each swing of her head. She was always vigilant and often shy around men, especially guys like Taylor. But she found herself attracted to him. Her mind was saying 'no,' but her body was screaming 'yes!'

Eyes on the counselors and campers, she said, "I don't know about this. Regina and Oscar already saw us. Don't you think they might tell someone?"

Taylor shrugged and said, "I don't care who they tell."

"Well, *I* do, you douchebag."

"You know that's not how I meant it. I was... I was just trying... Listen, I care about you and your reputation or whatever, but I care about *us* more. I just want us to spend some time together. That's what couples do, Carol. It's okay if you don't want to, I'm not gonna drag you through the woods like some monster, but... *if* you want to, now's our chance. You know, we're not going to get an opportunity like this for the rest of the summer. This... This is it, baby."

Carol nibbled on her bottom lip and cocked her head to the side as she looked him up and down, searching for a hint of deception. He seemed sincere, though—*cocky* but sincere. She hadn't caught him in a

CAMP BLAZE

AUTHOR'S ENHANCED EDITION

JON ATHAN

For more information on this book or the author, please visit
www.jon-athan.com. General inquiries are welcome.

Facebook: https://www.facebook.com/AuthorJonAthan
Twitter: @Jonny_Athan
Instagram: @AuthorJonnyAthan
Email: info@jon-athan.com

Cover illustration by Pedro Bianchi Guerra: https://www.
artstation.com/predo
Front cover typography and logo by: https://miblart.com/
Proofreading provided by Karen Bennett: kbennett4653@gmail.com

ISBN: 9798505694794

Second Edition

OTHER SLASHER NOVELS BY JON ATHAN

WARNING

This book contains scenes of intense violence and some disturbing themes. Some parts of this book may be considered violent, cruel, disturbing, or unusual. This book is *not* intended for those easily offended or appalled. Please enjoy at your own discretion.

CONTENTS

single lie since the beginning of camp, either. He was obviously looking to get his dick wet, but he didn't look like the type of guy to lie his way into sex.

Taylor was a charming young man. He wore the standard counselor uniform, but he opted for dark green trousers instead of shorts. His feathery black hair was combed over to the right. His chiseled, lean face was beardless, smooth and clean. He was a lean, strong young man with a big heart. He longed for sex like a virgin teenager in a raunchy comedy, but his love was genuine.

Carol smiled and said, "Fine. But I don't want to go out too far. If we get lost, everyone will have to come looking for us. It would be *too* embarrassing. I can't handle that. Like, I think I would *die* if that happened."

Grinning from ear to ear, Taylor grabbed her hand and said, "Don't worry about it. We won't be far from camp."

He gently pulled on his girlfriend's arm and led her into the woods. Carol couldn't help but blush as she followed him. The couple wandered the dark forest in search of a small shed.

Gusts of wind swept through the woods, whooshing and whistling with each puff. The trees groaned as if crying out in pain after being whipped by the harsh wind. The leaves swished and the bushes rustled, too. The music of nature echoed through the forest. The noise was loud and ceaseless, but it felt peaceful. An air of normality hung over the woods.

Taylor's eyes widened upon spotting a shed wedged between two trees. The twelve-by-twelve toolshed looked like it was barely standing, but it remained stable. As a matter of fact, the shed had been on the campgrounds for two decades without incident. It was a well-known getaway spot for counselors, passed down from one horny generation to another.

Taylor peeked into the shed through the windows and said, "Looks clear. Come on."

As she studied the rickety shed, concern written on her face, Carol asked, "Are you sure about this?"

"What do you mean?"

"I mean, are you sure you want to go in there?"

"Why not? What could go wrong?"

"Are you kidding me? Jeez, I don't know, Taylor. Oh wait, maybe the ceiling will *fall* on us? Maybe the windows will *shatter* and the glass will cut us up?"

Taylor chuckled, then he said, "Shut up and trust me."

He grabbed Carol's clammy hand and pulled her through the double-door entrance of the shed. As the doors closed behind them, the young man reached into the air. He smiled upon finding the beaded pull chain. With a good tug of the chain, the light bulb dangling from the ceiling lit up and a wave of yellow light washed over them.

Carol grimaced in disgust as she glanced around the small room. Dust danced in the air, slowly spiraling to the ground. There were several shelves on the walls to the right and left. A sturdy workbench hugged the wall directly in front of her. Layers of dust covered the tools; they looked like they hadn't been used in months, but most of the equipment still functioned properly. Axes, screwdrivers, pitchforks, cordless drills, heavy rope, and other supplies filled the tiny room.

Her brow raised, Carol asked, "This is the romantic spot you've been talking about this whole time? Is this some sort of joke?"

As he swiped the sawdust off of the workbench with the back of his hand, Taylor said, "I never said it was 'romantic.' I said it was a secret. There's a difference."

"You tricked me."

"No, no. Really, I think you just got confused. 'A secret can be romantic,' that's what I said. Remember?"

"No, actually, I don't."

Carol crossed her arms, puckered her lips, and turned away from him. She wasn't really angry, though. She was being playful—and Taylor could see right through her. He wrapped his arms around her waist and lifted her from the floor.

"Taylor!" Carol screamed, giggling. "Oh my God, my head's going to go through the roof!"

Taylor carried her over to the other end of the shed. He sat her on the workbench and gazed into her eyes. Her cheeks reddened, her nose twitched, and her eyes swiveled in their sockets.

Taylor said, "You're so beautiful."

Carol huffed, then she said, "Oh, *please*. I barely had enough time to get ready. Kenneth was in a hurry to go to the campfire, so Regina was really on our asses. I didn't have time to get, you know... I just didn't have time."

"You don't need time."

Carol giggled, then she asked, "And what's that supposed to mean?"

"It means when we're together, time doesn't matter. Time stops. We, uh... We move into our own little world. Makeup, muscles, all that shit that people say is beautiful... It's irrelevant to us. It's just you and me now, and we're perfect for each other the way we are."

Carol's cheeks couldn't get any redder. She lowered her head and stared down at her thighs. Taylor put his index finger on her chin and lifted her head. Before they could say another word, the couple kissed. Carol wrapped her arms around Taylor's neck while Taylor grabbed her hips. He kissed her chin, cheek, and her neck as he unfastened the buttons on her shirt. Lost in the moment, Carol could only let out a moan of pleasure.

"Wait," Carol whispered. Eyes growing, she squirmed on the workbench and asked, "What was that? Hey, Taylor, *what was that?*"

Baffled, Taylor stepped back and asked, "What? What is it?"

"I think there's someone out there."

Taylor smacked his lips, then he said, "*Come on, Carol.* There's no one outside. You're just nervous. And I get it, but you don't have to worry about a thing. I'll take–"

Shh—Carol held her index finger to her lips and shushed him as she stared out the window to her right. The light from the toolshed barely penetrated the filmy glass and lit up the woods. The wind dragged a few leaves past the shed, but there was nothing out of the ordinary.

"It's just the trees," Taylor said in a quiet, under-standing tone. "The trees and the wind."

"No, I swear I heard a–"

They both gasped upon hearing a set of footsteps outside. They recognized the moist thudding sounds. Someone was walking around in the mud out there.

Taylor leaned forward, peered out the window, and muttered, "What the hell? Is... Is someone really out there?"

As she buttoned her shirt, Carol said, "Someone's watching us, Taylor. Shit, someone must have followed us."

Hands around his face, Taylor leaned forward until his nose touched the dirty window. He saw leaves swirling in the wind and bushes shaking like hula dancers. He didn't see anyone in the woods, though. There were no animals outside, either.

Without taking his eyes off the forest, Taylor said,

"Maybe it's Kenneth. Maybe he's trying to scare us or something. You know how he is."

"What if it's worse?" Carol asked.

Taylor turned to face her, visibly curious. *What or who could be worse than Kenneth?*

Carol swallowed the lump in her throat, then she said, "It could be Alvin, right? He'd fire us if he caught us messing around. It could even be... some of the campers. Crap, what if they followed us out here?"

"And what if they did? Who gives a shit, right?"

"*I do.* I mean, we'd be... I don't know, we'd be setting a bad example or something, wouldn't we?"

"Having sex is setting a bad example? It's natural, Carol. Trust me, it's nothing they haven't seen before. I've already caught most of these brats peeking into the showers for crying out loud. Hell, they've probably already seen *you* naked, too. It's no big deal."

Flustered, Carol shook her head and said, "I'm not having sex or making out or doing *anything* with you until we take those campers back to the campsite. And if it's not a bunch of kids, I'm not going to keep going if Kenneth or Alvin are out there waiting for us. I'm not putting on a show for some pervs, young or old."

"All right, all right. I'll go check it out myself. If it's a few kids, I'll walk them back to the path. If it's Kenneth, I'll kick his ass. If it's Alvin... good luck to you 'cause I'm going to book it."

Before he could walk away, Carol grabbed Taylor's arm and said, "Don't be stupid. Splitting up in the middle of the night with some creep out there? Are you joking? We have to be careful. You've seen the idiots in those horror movies, haven't you? We'll check it out together."

Taylor smiled as Carol marched forward. She was shy and reserved, especially when it came to intimate relationships, but she had the heart of a lion. He admired that about her. He loved every bit of her. He rubbed the nape of his neck, snickered, and followed her lead.

Carol crossed her arms and rubbed her shoulders as she scanned the forest. Between the trees in front of her, she could see some dim light coming from the camp's cabins. They weren't very far from the main campsite. She glanced back at the toolshed and examined the surrounding trees. She couldn't see much through the darkness.

Taylor walked to Carol's side and said, "I don't see anyone. Maybe it was just our imaginations or maybe... maybe somebody was just walking by. Probably didn't even know we were in there. Hell, it could have just been the wind like I said earlier. Come on, let's go back inside."

Carol grasped at Taylor's sleeve and said, "No. I heard someone, Taylor. I'm not going back in *there* while someone's out *here* watching us. Maybe we should just go back to the cabin or meet up with the others at the campfire."

"Carol, there is *no one* out here. Trust me."

She frowned and sniffled as she looked at the ground. She liked Taylor, she trusted him with all of her fragile little heart, but she couldn't smother her anxiety and ignore her fears. Mysteries raised questions and questions demanded answers. She refused to return to the secluded toolshed without some semblance of security.

Taylor could see the doubt lingering in Carol's eyes, too. He couldn't convince her with words, so he opted for actions.

He shouted, "Kenneth?! Are you out there? You messing with us, you damn perv?" There was no response. He yelled, "If I catch you, I'm gonna kick your ass! You hear me?!"

Carol hooked her arm over the crook of Taylor's elbow, snuggled up close to him, and whispered, "Hey, watch what you say. You might be threatening some kids. You don't want to get fired, do you?" She glanced around and said, "Um... Come on out, kids. You're not in any trouble, I promise."

Once again, there was no answer. The sounds of crackling leaves, groaning trees, and creaky wood echoed through the area. They had sought a little bit of privacy, but they found a terrible sense of seclusion in the woods instead. They felt like they were the last two people in the entire campsite.

Taylor rubbed Carol's hand and said, "You see? It's exactly like I said: *The wind*. Let's get back inside before anyone sees us out here."

Carol nodded reluctantly as she took one final glance into the woods. To her dismay, only the darkness stared back. The couple turned and stepped towards the toolshed.

Three steps.

They only took three steps before they were forced to stop. They stood less than three meters away from the shed's doors, frozen with fear.

Taylor stammered, "Wh–Who–Who... are you?"

A tall, brawny person stood on top of the toolshed, his large silhouette contrasting against the moon. He wore navy-hooded coveralls and white gloves. Some long, stray hairs stuck out from under the hood over his head. A white mask shielded his face and hid his identity. The mask had a blank expression, like a mannequin's face, but his shiny blue irises were visible through the eye holes.

The mysterious person's sudden appearance was worrisome. His weapon, however, made the counselors shudder with great fright. Fingers wrapped tightly around the wooden handle, he held a fire axe out in front of him.

Taylor held his hands up in a peaceful gesture and said, "Yo, man, if this is some sort of prank, you got us. All right? Ha-ha, very funny, *you win*. We're scared, we've learned our lesson, whatever. Come down from there before you hurt yourself or–or us. I, um... I know you don't want to do that. Right?" The man remained quiet. Taylor stuttered, "Ra–Right?"

The counselors recoiled as the masked person raised the axe overhead.

Eyes huge with terror, Carol grabbed Taylor's arm and said, "What is he–"

The masked person jumped off the toolshed and swung the axe down. The blade struck Taylor's face with an unnerving *crunch*. The man landed on his feet in front of him, the ground vibrating under his steel-toed boots. Carol wobbled away and shrieked. Her feet tangled, sending her plummeting to the ground.

Although the counselor stayed on his feet, legs shaking under him, the axe head split Taylor's face in half vertically down the middle—from his hairline to his upper lip. The blade broke through his skull and punctured his brain. His left eye drifted to the left while his other eye wandered to the right. His muti-lated nose was pushed *into* his skull.

Two of his upper incisor teeth were dislodged by the brutal blow, too. The detached teeth rode the thick string of bloody drool hanging from his mouth to the ground between his sneakers.

The masked person released his grip on the handle. Taylor took a step back, then turned unsteadily to face Carol. On the ground, Carol propped herself up on her elbows. She was about to lurch away when she saw Taylor's face. She gaped at him, her mouth open as wide as humanly possible. A paralyzing fear gripped her.

Taylor's face had been reduced to a bloody mass of crumpled flesh. Blood poured out of the massive gash in waves, rippling across his cheeks and dripping from his jaw like a crimson waterfall. A moment ago, he was the most handsome man she had ever met. Now, she couldn't recognize him. She shrieked as he fell towards her.

Upon hitting the ground face-first, the axe went deeper into Taylor's skull. Blood began to ooze out of his ear canals.

Carol scrambled to the closest shelter—*the toolshed*. She considered running into the woods to find the other counselors, but she felt like her legs were moving on autopilot. Her survival instincts told her to find a safe place to fortify.

Hide, her inner voice said. *Barricade yourself!*

She stumbled into the toolshed. She noticed the killer wasn't running after her. She closed the doors behind her and reached for a lock, but she found herself grasping at the air. A horrifying realization hit her: The doors only locked from the outside. She looked to her left, then to her right, searching for a way to barricade herself inside.

Then her eyes shrank to slits upon hearing a set of hurried footsteps. And the footsteps grew louder and louder. Her eyes bugged out as she began to step back, but she was too late.

The doors burst open. The edge of one of the doors collided with her face, leaving a small but deep cut on the bridge of her nose. Disoriented, Carol tottered back. She fell over the workbench at the end of the cramped room, blood dripping from her nostrils. A thick vein stuck out from the center of her rosy forehead.

She mumbled, "Plee–Please... Please... Don–Don't hur... hurt me. Please, please, plee–please..."

The masked killer stood in the doorway, remarkably calm and confident. Taylor's violent death and Carol's weak pleas for mercy didn't bother him. He was at a busy camp filled with counselors and campers, but he looked like he wasn't afraid of being caught. It was all premeditated—all part of the plan.

He approached the shelves to his right and examined his arsenal of deadly tools. He grabbed the heavy rope, then moseyed over to Carol's side.

"N–No," she said weakly as he wrapped one arm around her waist. "Please don't. Please, I–I'm begging you. Please."

The killer lifted her from the floor, then tossed her onto the workbench. She groaned as she landed on her back. She twisted and turned, blindly kicking and punching the air, but she couldn't escape the killer's clutches. He tied her wrists together with the heavy rope, then he pulled her arms overhead. With the other end of the rope, he tied her to the workbench.

The masked person returned to the shelves. Carol

attempted to roll off the workbench. One of her legs fell off, but she was too short to reach the floor. She shimmied closer to the edge.

"I–I don't wanna die," she whimpered. "I–I–I can't die. I don't wanna die. Don't do this. God, don–don't let him do this."

Her eyes—glazed with tears—grew to the size of golf balls as the killer approached the workbench with a cordless power drill in one hand. Her throat and mouth completely dried. She couldn't speak, so she screamed.

With his free hand, the killer unbuttoned her shorts. She kicked him, leaving an imprint of her shoe on his burly chest, but she didn't hurt him. He pulled her shorts off and threw them to the floor. Her white underwear—lace panties she wore just for Taylor—followed, revealing her trimmed pubic hair.

"No!" Carol shouted in a hoarse tone. "No! No! *No!*"

The killer raised the power drill up to her face and squeezed the trigger. The flat wood drill bit spun quickly. The drill's buzzing competed with Carol's strained vocal cords.

Thrashing on the workbench, Carol cried, "I'm begging you! Don't kill me! Please! I don't wanna die! God, no! Please!"

The killer released the trigger and gazed into Carol's eyes. He tilted his head from side to side, as if he were studying her.

"Please," Carol repeated, a web of tears around her eyes.

The killer huffed. Carol squealed as he forced her legs open. She didn't have the opportunity to put up a fight. It all happened so fast. The air was vacuumed from her lungs as the masked psychopath shoved the drill bit into her vagina. He gazed into her wide, bulging eyes for a moment to appreciate her fear—to absorb it, to devour it like a full-course meal.

Then he squeezed the trigger.

A BLOODCURDLING SCREAM ECHOED THROUGH THE DARK forest, joining the groaning tree branches, rustling leaves, and crackling flames. It blew past the campfire like a gust of wind.

Regina Park, the head counselor, glanced over her shoulder and peered into the cluttered trees behind her. There was a tremendous concern in her dark eyes.

Not the wind, she thought. *An animal?*

"You hear that?" Kenneth Wolf asked, his hand up to his ear.

Regina turned in her seat and followed his voice. He sat directly across from her. She could see his smug smile through the dancing flames between them. His spiky hair looked like a field of horns on his head. She smiled thinly and shook her head, communicating without saying a word: '*No scary stories.*' At heart, however, she knew she wasn't really in command. She couldn't stop Kenneth without annoying the campers and she didn't want to turn them against her.

A large group of kids surrounded the campfire, sitting on foldable chairs and tree trunks. The youngest in the group was nine years old and the oldest was twelve. They looked frightened—brows scrunched, shoulders raised, arms crossed, hands up to their mouths—*but interested*. Campfires, s'mores, and scary stories were summer camp traditions. And Kenneth spent most of his teenage summers in places like Camp Blaze, so he respected tradition.

He wagged his pointer finger and said, "A few of the counselors here—*like Regina*—probably don't want me to tell you this story."

Regina laughed and rolled her eyes as some of the campers booed at her. A couple of the kids gave her a thumbs-down gesture, too.

"C'mon, tell the story!" a boy yelled.

Another boy said, "Do it, Kenny."

"Don't," a little girl squeaked out.

No one heard her over the campers' clamoring, though.

"All right, all right," Kenneth said, hands up as if he were surrendering to the police. It took the children some thirty seconds to quiet down. Kenneth said, "You didn't let me finish. Regina might not want me to tell you, but... I'm going to tell you anyway."

"Yes!" one of the boys exclaimed.

Regina grunted to capture the group's attention,

then she said, "Kenny, I know you love—I mean, really *love*—these stories, but I don't think it's appropriate." She glanced at the young man sitting next to her and asked, "Isn't that right, Oscar?"

Oscar Orozco, another senior counselor, smiled nervously. He looked down, ran his fingers through his slick hair, then massaged the nape of his neck. Truth be told, he didn't mind Kenneth's stories. He loved horror movies and urban legends after all. He glanced at Kenneth, then back at Regina. He felt like a child stuck between his arguing parents who had just asked him who he loved more.

Side with the douchebag or with my girlfriend, he thought.

He shrugged at Regina and said, "A scary story never hurt anyone."

Regina sighed, then she said, "Okay, do whatever you want, guys."

The campers responded with a cheer of approval: '*Hurray!*'

"Perfect," Kenneth said as he clapped, a grin contorting his young, smooth face. He said, "But Regina... Hey, listen up, okay? Regina's right. This story might be 'inappropriate' for some of you. So, if you get scared, close your eyes *real* tight, hold your hands over your ears, and keep repeating this phrase: 'It's only a story... only a story... only a story.' Got it?"

As the campers giggled and fidgeted in their seats, eager to hear the tale, Kenneth looked around the forest. An impenetrable darkness swallowed the woods. The moonlight could hardly pierce the dense trees. The campfire, crackling and popping, provided a ring of illumination, washing their bodies with a dark orange glow. It was the only source of warmth out there, too.

Kenneth gazed at the fire and said, "That scream you heard... That wasn't the wind. It wasn't–"

"It *was* the wind," Regina interrupted.

The kids booed her again.

Kenneth shushed the campers, then he said, "It's okay, it's all right. She's not going to interrupt again. Isn't that right, Regina?"

Regina rubbed her temple and forced a smile. Her intentions were pure. She could tolerate urban legends, but she didn't want the kids to fear *their* camp. She couldn't win against Kenneth, though. She pulled her lips into her mouth and gave him a nod.

"Perfect," Kenneth said. "Now, that scream you heard... That wasn't the wind. It wasn't a tree or a bush in the woods. Wasn't a big bad bear or a mountain lion. No, *that* was one of Ash Palmer's victims. You probably all heard about Ash before you got here, right? Your parents told you he wasn't real. Maybe they said he was just a... a made-up boogeyman. Well, kids, they lied to you."

A chubby twelve-year-old boy raised his hand and stuttered, "I–I... I heard this story before. My big brother told me. Isn't, um... Ash is dead, isn't he?"

"You are correct. Everyone knows little Ash Palmer is... dead. They say he drowned in the lake, but, seriously, they say that about every kid who dies at summer camp. Do you wanna know how he really died? You wanna know the truth?"

The child lowered his hand and gulped.

Kenneth snickered, then he said, "Well, we have to go back to 1975 for that story—26 years ago. On a night like this, Ash was minding his own business. He was playing outside, collecting bugs and looking at rocks. Then a couple of counselors led him away from his cabin. They promised him some sweets. You know, they say Ash had a sweet tooth. He really loved cake and candy. And he trusted those counselors. I mean, they were *counselors* after all. He wasn't wrong to trust them. But... these counselors weren't like me, like Regina, like any of us. They were different."

"What was wrong with them?" a girl asked.

"They worshipped a *demon*. They were cult members. Their demon was hungry, you see? So, they needed a sacrifice. They took Ash to a campfire like this one and they tied him to a log in the fire pit. Then..."

Kenneth paused to check on the children and build some tension. He was pleased to see he had their undivided attention.

He said, "Then they lit him on fire. He burned to death that night. And trust me, kids, you don't know pain until you *burn*. His skin came off first, then his

muscles started cooking. His eyes, too. Those just...
melted. The whites of his eyes went down his cheeks
like... like watery egg whites. Like your breakfast, you
know?"

"Kenneth," Regina said in a quiet but stern voice.
"Tone it down."

Some of the younger kids didn't understand every
detail. The older kids were starting to squirm and
whimper, though.

Kenneth said, "My point is: He suffered. The counselors were arrested, the camp was closed, and Ash's
parents were left with... nothing but Ash's ashes."

He chuckled, amused by his own wordplay. Regina
sneered in disgust while some of the other counselors
gasped. Some of the campers closed their eyes, tucked
their chins between their knees, and followed
Kenneth's advice, lips moving in a silent chant: '*Only a
story... Only a story... Only a story.*' A handful of
campers remained attentive.

The story wasn't over yet.

Kenneth said, "The camp reopened a few years later.
I think it was May 9th, 1980. And everything went back
to normal. Sunny summer days playing on obstacle
courses, swimming at the lake, hiking through the
woods... until 1988. That's when things got interesting
—*really* interesting. Counselors started disappearing,
vanishing without a trace. *Poof!*" Some of the campers
flinched, then giggled in relief. Kenneth continued, "A

few campers disappeared, too. And it wasn't until the end of that summer that they finally found the missing kids. All of them were... *dead*. They say they were burned to death. And you wanna know who did it?"

He noticed some slight nods from his audience of campers. A couple of kids responded with soft whimpers. He saw expressions of annoyance and worry on some of the other counselors.

Time to wrap it up, he thought.

He said, "They say... the killer was... a boy without skin... a boy with a whole lot of experience with fire... a boy named *Ash Palmer*. He's still out here looking for revenge, too. It's the 26th anniversary of his death this year. I heard he killed 13 people back in 1988. Who knows? He might come back and kill 26 of us this year."

Regina's disgust turned into discomfort. She had heard the story of Ash Palmer dozens of times before, but it never grew on her. She couldn't understand why anyone would want to hear about a child's violent death. From right to left, she observed the other counselors and campers. Some were enthusiastic, others were bored, and most were scared shitless.

"That's enough scary stories for one night," Regina said. "Let's get you all to bed."

About half of the children responded with a groan of disappointment. Some of them were frightened by Kenneth's tale, but they would rather spend time with friends and listen to scary stories than sleep. The other half breathed a sigh of relief.

Kenneth said, "It's still early. I think we have time for one more."

"No."

"Seriously? Okay, I'll work with you. I'll tell something a little less–"

"I said no, Kenneth. You're not going to stay up with them if they have nightmares. *I am*. Let's go."

She sprung to her feet, turned on her flashlight, and beckoned to the campers. The kids and counselors followed her lead while Kenneth stayed behind to extinguish the fire.

Regina walked backwards in front of two parallel lines of campers, occasionally glancing over her shoulder to avoid tripping over herself. The kids held hands while counselors walked beside them at regular intervals.

"You should get back in line before someone gets hurt," Regina said as Oscar jogged towards her.

Oscar slowed to a stroll next to her. He smiled at the kids at the front of the line, then huffed as he turned his attention to Regina.

He said, "They can walk in a straight line without us watching them."

"I wasn't talking about the kids."

"Oh, *really?* And who's going to hurt me? Huh?

You?"

"I'd be careful if I were you. I'm not the top dog for nothing. I had to fight my way to get here."

"The only thing you're fighting out here is mosquitoes."

Regina smirked and said, "And those mosquitoes are a lot tougher than you."

Oscar responded with an exaggerated laugh: "Ha-ha-*ha!*"

He gazed into Regina's dark brown eyes. Although her irises looked black in the night, her eyes glimmered like the stars above them. Her black hair touched her narrow shoulders, silky and straight. Her tender smiles—no matter how slight—always created deep dimples in her cheeks. In Oscar's eyes, she was the most beautiful woman he had ever seen, inside and out.

"Why didn't you want to stick around back there?" Oscar asked. "I mean, Kenny was right. We had time for another story, didn't we?"

"We did," Regina responded as she turned around and continued walking. "I just don't like his stories."

"None of them? You told the Hookman urban legend last year, didn't you? He tells that one sometimes, too."

"Okay, I meant to say: I don't like *that* story. *That* awful story that he always has to tell for some reason."

"Ash's story?"

Regina nodded.

Oscar asked, "Why?"

"Because it's real. Ash obviously didn't come back to life and kill those people in '88. That's the 'urban legend' part of the story. But that first part was true. Ash Palmer isn't some made-up monster—some boogeyman—created to scare kids at camp. He was a *real* kid who suffered from a *real* death. It's not a fun story when you know the truth."

Oscar said, "Damn. I didn't know. My big bro told me the story when I was a kid. I, um..." He laughed inwardly, then he said, "I started crying so much because I didn't want to come here anymore. I even tried hiding under my bed when it was time to go. So, my brother told me he made it all up. 'I was fucking with you,' he said. I guess he was just lying to make me feel better."

"He probably didn't know it was real, either."

"Well, I'm... I'm sorry. I shouldn't have let Kenny tell that story."

Ignoring the apology, Regina peeked over her shoulder and shouted, "Hawks! Here's your stop! Get in there, brush your teeth, and get ready for bed! Chop-chop!"

She clapped as the girls and boys ran into the cabins in the section. The camp's living quarters were split into three groups with two cabins each—one for the boys, one for the girls. The *Hawks* resided in the northeast side of the camp, the *Gators* occupied the southeast area near the lake, and the *Bears* lived in the woods between the other groups. A single wide dirt path connected all of the cabins.

Towards the middle of it, the dirt path branched out and led to the counselors' cabin, which was located farther west. It was a two-story building. There were eight bedrooms on the second floor—four for the women, four for the men. The first floor served as a private recreational area for the counselors. Campers were not allowed to enter the building.

Towards the center of the camp, a strip of log buildings stretched from the main road to the lake. The administration building, cafeteria, recreation hall, large pavilion, and quad were located in that area.

As they reached the second set of cabins, Regina cupped her hands around her mouth and yelled, "Bears! Get in there and get ready for bed! C'mon now, we don't have all night!"

The other kids kept chatting and bantering and roughhousing as they headed towards the last cabins.

Regina furrowed her brow upon spotting a dark figure ahead of them. Her shoulders inched up to her ears as a rush of anxiety spread through her body. *A counselor? A trespasser?* she thought as she attempted to identify the figure from afar. With each step, she got a better view of the person. Skinny and frail, he plodded towards them. A powerful gust of wind could have plucked him from the ground like a dandelion. Her shoulders dropped as the man stopped under a lamppost.

It was Alvin Perry. He was the proud owner of Camp Blaze. Like his counselors and campers, the elderly man wore a camp uniform. He wore a green windbreaker jacket over his button-up shirt, though. His thin white hair was combed over a bald spot at the center of his scalp. His skin was gnarled like a tree trunk but flabby like a turkey's snood. But he exuded a youthful, sprightly aura. He still believed in the magic of summer camp.

Alvin waved at the group and asked, "How was the campfire, kiddos? Tell plenty of scary stories?"

"Yes, Mr. Perry!" the kids shouted in unison.

Alvin smiled and said, "Wonderful. Now, you all have a good night. And don't let the bedbugs bite. If they do, you tell me and ol' Uncle Perry will bite them back."

He chomped at the air and growled playfully. Some of the kids giggled and ran around him.

"I wanna eat a bedbug, too!" one of the boys shouted.

"Eww," a girl said. "I hate bugs!"

As the kids marched past him, Alvin said, "Regina, do you have a minute?"

"Sure, I think Matt and the others can handle these little troublemakers without me. What's on your mind, Mr. Perry?"

Regina and Oscar stopped in front of the old man.

Alvin said, "Well, I've been trying to contact Taylor on his radio for the past hour and I haven't heard back from him. I told him he was needed at the cafeteria tonight and he didn't show up. Have you seen him?"

"No, um... No, I haven't seen him."

"No? He didn't head out with you?"

Regina's gaze dropped to the ground. She had an *idea* of Taylor's location. She had watched him and Carol enter the woods earlier that night after all. She didn't want to throw them under the bus, but she was an honest person—a *very* honest person. The mere thought of lying made her anxiety spike.

Oscar said, "He's probably with Carol, sir."

"Is that so? Did I assign them to something else?"

"Probably not. They're a... They're a couple, sir. If I can be honest with you, they're probably out there messing around. I wouldn't worry about them. I wouldn't be too hard on them, either. You were young once, right?"

"I was young, but I wasn't reckless," Alvin responded. "They shouldn't be 'messing around' while on the clock, especially with all of these kids around. And it's nighttime, too. They could fall and hurt themselves out there. They could be hurt or in danger at this very moment. Now I'm going to have to call a ranger and see if we can get a search party started."

"You're right, Mr. Perry," Regina said. "I'll talk to them about this when they get back, but I really don't think a search party is necessary. Taylor and Carol know these woods very well, so I'm sure they're fine. A search party would just bring them a lot of unwanted attention, and that would just humiliate them in front of everyone. Besides, they'll probably be back before we could even get a search party organized."

"Are you sure?"

Oscar said, "I can go out there and look for 'em if you want."

Regina said, "I can help, too. But I honestly feel like it would be best if we just waited for them here. There's no reason for all of us to be running through the woods at night. Plus, like I said, I don't think it would be good for them or anyone if we caught them... in the 'act,' if you know what I mean."

"*Hmm,*" Alvin hummed as he considered his options.

Oscar said, "She means sex, sir. It wouldn't be good for them if we caught them having–"

"I know what she means," Alvin interrupted, a smile playing at the corners of his mouth. "Okay, we'll let them be—*for now*. But as soon as they get back, I want you to make sure they understand the rules, Regina. You too, Oscar. No more 'messing around' or whatnot on the clock. It is completely inappropriate. Are we clear?"

"Yes, Mr. Perry," Regina answered.

Oscar said, "Crystal clear, sir."

Alvin clasped his hands behind his back and, as he lumbered away, he said, "Let me know if they're not back by dawn. I'll have to call the rangers then."

"I'll keep you updated," Regina said.

She glanced over at Oscar and shrugged, then she marched forward. Oscar followed her lead. From a distance, they could see the last few campers running into the Gators' cabins while a few junior counselors supervised them from outside.

Oscar asked, "You think Taylor will get fired this time?"

"Nope. You know Alvin. He isn't *that* strict. He'll scold him, he'll act disappointed, but he won't punish them. Well, he won't fire them. We can expect to see them working in the kitchen for the next few weeks, but it won't be too bad."

"Kitchen duty? That's it? That doesn't sound bad at all. Why don't we go out and, um... have a little fun ourselves?"

Regina turned to face him and said, "Because it's bedtime and I'm sleepy." She kissed him, then she said, "Good night, babe. See you tomorrow."

"We're going to the same cabin. We can still talk and hang out, y'know?"

Regina looked back and winked at him, but she kept walking. A smile bloomed on Oscar's face as he watched her stroll to the counselors' cabin. Her movements, albeit normal, captivated him. He blushed, like a child flirting with his crush for the first time. He truly cared about her.

"God, I love this girl," he whispered as he followed her to the cabin.

3

THE MOST IMPORTANT MEAL

THE DELIGHTFUL SCENT OF BREAKFAST POURED OUT OF the kitchen's pass-through window and swept through the cafeteria. The campers chose from a menu of breakfast favorites: Scrambled eggs, pancakes, waffles, sausage, bacon, peanut butter and jelly sandwiches, cereal, and fruit cups. The kids drank orange juice and milk while the counselors sipped on their coffee.

Savoring the room's cheerful atmosphere, Regina stood with her hands on her hips in the center aisle, smack-dab between two rows of wooden cafeteria tables. A couple of counselors sang classic camp songs with the younger kids. At the moment, they were singing a tuneless rendition of *Kumbaya*. The rest of the kids were eating and chatting. Some of them even negotiated trades for their breakfast.

'*Half of my peanut butter sandwich for one of your mini pancakes.*'

Regina wasn't too pleased with the cliques in the cafeteria. The kids were separated into different groups for the sake of organization and friendly competition. Their programs were designed to promote friendship amongst the campers, though. Yet, cliques seemed to be part of human nature. They couldn't stop the kids from creating their own little exclusive clubs.

She sucked her teeth upon spotting a lonesome camper—*Kimberly Morgan.*

At twelve years old, Kimberly was one of the older kids at Camp Blaze. She had been at the camp before, she knew some of the other campers from previous summers, but she was a devout introvert. A group of kids sat at the table next to her, they had invited her to chat, but she remained distant and silent. She wasn't bullied by the other kids. She just didn't know how to be sociable.

Her downcast eyes drifted to the food on her plate. She twirled her blonde hair and stabbed her waffle with her plastic spork.

Regina sat next to her and said, "Hey, Kim. How's it going?"

"Okay," Kimberly responded in a monotone voice.

"Okay?"

"Yeah, I'm okay."

"You haven't touched your food. Aren't you hungry?"

The young girl shrugged and said, "Not really."

"Why not, sweetie? You know breakfast is the most important meal of the day, right? It's, um... It's *fuel* for the body, y'know? You can't play later if you don't eat now."

"I know, but... I don't know. I'm just not that hungry, I guess. Maybe I'll eat more during lunch or something, but... not now. Sorry."

Regina pouted. Smiles were contagious but so was sadness. She could feel the girl's loneliness. The rest of the camp was bathed in sunshine, but this girl had a black cloud over her head.

She stroked Kimberly's hair and said, "You don't have to apologize for that. As long as you're feeling okay, it's not a big deal. Breakfast is important—it's very important—but I won't and can't force you to eat. Just promise me you'll grab a bite to eat at lunchtime, okay?"

"I promise," Kimberly said, smiling slightly.

"Good. You're not starving under my watch, squirt."

"Yeah, I won't."

She laughed a little. She didn't have many friends at the camp, but she liked Regina. They couldn't be the best of friends because of their age difference, but they shared a sisterly bond.

Kimberly asked, "What are we doing today?"

"The obstacle course."

"Can I... Is it okay if I skip the obstacle course today?"

Regina examined the girl from head to toe and toe to head. She was worried about her isolation and lack of appetite. She feared she wasn't telling her the truth. *Maybe she caught a cold,* she thought. *Or maybe she's just very, very shy.*

She asked, "Are you sure you're okay, Kim? If you're feeling under the weather or anything like that, you know we're here to help you, right?"

"Yeah, yeah, I know," Kimberly said, smiling nervously. "I'm okay, really."

Regina pressed the back of her hand against Kimberly's forehead to check her temperature. The girl was warm, but she didn't have a fever.

The counselor said, "Yeah, you seem fine. You're just... You're acting a little funny today, kiddo. Why don't you want to go on the obstacle course? It's a lot of fun and everyone's going to be there."

"That's why."

"Hmm?"

"That's why I don't wanna go. *Everyone* is going. I just don't like being with so many people. It's... scary. I can't talk to them and I don't know if they even want to talk to me."

Regina said, "I get what you're saying. But you don't have to worry about that. You just stick with me, okay? Anyone who talks to me will have to talk to you. And I'll be right there by your side every step of the way. You don't have to take any big steps by yourself. What do you think about that? Sound good?"

"I guess it's okay."

"Regina!" Alvin hollered from the cafeteria's entrance. He beckoned to her and said, "We need to talk. *Now.*"

"I'll be right there, sir!"

Kimberly said, "He sounds angry."

Regina responded, "Probably didn't get his waffles this morning. You should eat yours before he comes over here and gobbles 'em up." She stood up and said, "Seriously, try to eat a little. And bring a granola bar with you to the obstacle course. I don't want you fainting out there. It's only going to get hotter later."

"Okay," Kimberly said before taking a bite of her waffle.

"Attagirl. See you soon, kiddo."

———

Regina squinted as the bright morning sunshine flashed in her eyes. She held her arm over her forehead and looked to her right. She saw the quad out there—an outdoor seating area with two columns of benches, like pews in a church. The foyer of the camp and the administration building were located just beyond those benches.

Alvin paced between the quad and cafeteria, muttering indistinctly to himself as he tapped away at his flip phone. It took him a long time to type a simple text message with the numeric keypad.

As she approached him, Regina said, "Hey, Mr. Perry, what's up?"

Alvin stopped walking. He slammed the phone shut, then he wagged it at the counselor. Regina had rarely seen him so flustered.

"I haven't heard from him," Alvin said.

"Who?"

"Mr. Taylor Harris. You said Taylor was... 'messing around.' Now, how long does that usually take? Hmm? Wait, don't... don't answer that."

Regina shut her eyes and shook her head, as if to say: '*No way.*' She asked, "He's not back yet?"

"I have no idea. I've been running around in circles trying to get ahold of him, but... *nada.* I've checked the cabins, checked the lake, just came out of the kitchen, but he's nowhere to be found. I'll be honest with you. I'm trying to keep this whole thing a secret so it doesn't frighten all of the campers and blow up in our faces. Panic won't help anyone. I'm sure you'll agree with me. But... I'm worried, Regina."

"I understand, sir. I'm worried, too. Come to think of it, I didn't see Carol this morning, either. She wasn't in bed, wasn't in the shower, wasn't in the cafeteria. Taylor is usually with Oscar in the mornings, but I didn't see them together. Maybe... Are you sure he wasn't in the kitchen? I saw some of the guys in there earlier."

Alvin sucked his teeth and shook his head, communicating without saying a word: '*He wasn't there.'* Regina started orbiting the old man while rubbing her chin. Pessimistic thoughts—visions of tragedy—flooded her mind. *A romance gone wrong,* she thought. She pictured Taylor murdering Carol after she rejected him, dumping her body in the lake, then running off into the woods.

Interrupting her thoughts, Alvin said, "I don't want this to spread. I can see it in your eyes, little lady. This isn't a story from one of your romance books. This is a serious emergency. Now, are you sure—absolutely positive—that you saw them leave together on a little 'escapade?' You're not lying to me, are you?"

"Of course not, sir. We told you the truth last night. We were walking to the campfire with the kids. Oscar and I saw Taylor and Carol at the back of the line. I went back to tell them to catch up. They... Look, they asked me if it was okay for them to ditch the campfire. I thought it would be fine since they have experience in the woods and we had more than enough counselors with us to take care of the kids. That's my fault. This is *all* my fault. I'm sorry."

"Don't worry about that right now. Where did they go, Regina?"

"I'm not sure. They either went to the shore, the boathouse, or the toolshed in the woods."

Alvin said, "So, they could have drowned, hurt themselves with the power tools, or stole a boat." He sighed, then in a blatantly sarcastic tone, he said, "*Great.*"

While Alvin muttered to himself, Regina said, "I really didn't think it would turn out like this. They're a couple. They're... 'official.' They're not just some love-birds who wanted to mess around. They weren't caught up in the moment or anything like that. They've been talking about moving in together after camp. They're serious and I... I thought I was doing them a favor."

Alvin saw the regret in Regina's eyes. He couldn't blame her. He was a sucker for romance, too. Throughout his years at Camp Blaze, he had seen many relationships blossom. Some of his counselors went on to get married. He assumed, if they truly loved each other, that Taylor and Carol were safe together.

He said, "They're probably fine, but I can't ignore this. So, whether they're messing around or not, I'm calling the authorities. I want them found as soon as possible. Now, please wait here for a moment. This darn thing doesn't get a signal in this area. If I need anything from you, I'll holler."

Alvin waved at Regina as he walked away. Regina crossed her arms and watched the owner wander around the quad, swinging his phone around in search of reception. It took him about three minutes just to contact the police. She could only hear bits and pieces of the conversation. She found some comfort in Alvin's calm demeanor, though. He was worried, but he wasn't hysterical.

His confident, caring leadership made her feel secure. Camp Blaze was in good hands.

"What happened?" Regina asked as Alvin closed his phone and approached her.

"They're sending a unit in an hour or two."

"That's it? Just one patrol car?"

Alvin nodded and said, "I want you to keep this quiet. Just follow the regular schedule for the rest of the day. You're going to the obstacle course later, correct?"

"Ye–Yeah," Regina faltered. She grunted to clear her throat, then she said, "We're heading out in the next thirty, forty-five minutes or so. Something like that. When we get back, we're, um… we're giving the kids an option between archery at the range and arts and crafts in the quad."

"Good. Stick to that schedule. Try to keep the kids away from that shed and the boathouse in case the cops have to investigate or whatnot. And don't tell anyone about this. I don't want this place to go crazy with rumors."

"No problem, sir. I can handle it."

As he walked away, Alvin waved and said, "See you in a few, Regina."

Regina watched him as he made his way through the quad, then she looked back at the cafeteria. She heard the kids chatting and giggling in there. She saw the building as a big powder keg. She knew a single word about the mysterious disappearances would ignite an explosion of madness and panic amongst the campers and counselors. She was afraid to think about what Kenneth would do if he caught wind of the situation.

He'd be there fanning the flames, she thought.

She took a deep breath, then she whispered, "Act natural. Stay on schedule. Everything's fine."

4

THE OBSTACLE COURSE

Walking backwards, Regina clapped and shouted, "Be careful, ladies and gentlemen! Try to keep your balance but don't hurt yourselves! You know what we say: *Safety* before *bravery!* If you fall, pick yourselves up, get to the back of the line, and try again. If you get any cuts, go straight to a counselor. All right, c'mon, you can do this!" She glanced at the girl at the front of the line—*Kimberly*. She winked at her and said, "Told you it would be fun, kiddo."

Kimberly's gentle laughter could melt the coldest heart. Arms outstretched for balance, she made her way onto an elevated plank of wood—a makeshift balance beam. She leaned to her left and looked at the muddy ground some seven inches below her. It was a short, harmless fall, but it still excited her. It reminded her of the good times she shared with her older sister years ago, climbing the furniture in the living room as they pretended the floor was hot lava.

"I bet I can make it all the way to the end without starting over," Kimberly said with a bright smile.

Regina was relieved to see the black cloud over the girl's head had been blown away. Emotions were like the weather—often predictable, occasionally surprising, always changing.

"Oh, *really?*" Regina asked, bug-eyed. "It's only been done by a few campers in the past, sport. A few strong, hardworking campers. Did you know that?"

"Yup."

Regina pointed at herself with her thumbs and said, "And *I'm* one of those campers. You think you can beat my record? Hmm? You think you can beat the master?"

"Yup!" Kimberly said with more enthusiasm.

"All right, all right. We'll see about that, kiddo."

Regina turned to face forward. She walked on her tiptoes and took a gander at the rest of the obstacle course. The makeshift balance beams led to a crawling exercise. Like soldiers crawling under barbed wire, the campers were supposed to crawl under a cargo net made out of durable rope. The crawling activity led to a field of large tires where the kids had to lunge through them without falling over. The obstacle course came to an end at a short rock-climbing wall—four meters to the top, then a slide down to a pool of fluffy . pillows.

Years earlier, the obstacle course involved tightropes, tree-climbing, and swings, but those activities were removed due to several accidents.

"It's going to be tough, kid, but you can do it," Regina whispered. "I believe in you."

She stopped and looked back. She watched as the kids, laughing and chatting, walked past her. Some of the older boys tried to scare each other off the balance beam. Kimberly broke out of her shell to share a few words with Christina, the girl walking behind her. As usual, junior and senior counselors walked next to the campers at regular intervals, making sure they were all safe and sound. But some of them enjoyed roughhousing, too.

Oscar and Kenneth teased the campers, shaking the balance beams and screaming to frighten them. They weren't trying to bully the kids, though. They acted more like obnoxious older brothers than complete assholes. Some of the kids were annoyed by their actions and others welcomed the challenge. One of the girls even goaded them.

"You can't knock me off!" she said before sticking her tongue out at Kenneth.

Regina yelled, "You guys should hop on! I'm sure the kids would love to see you try this one!"

Kimberly looked back and shouted, "Yeah! Don't be scared!"

"They'd probably pee their pants," a curly-haired boy said.

"Very funny," Oscar said. "I've gone through this course a hundred times and I could go through it a hundred times more. As a matter of fact, I helped design it just for you '*lovely*' kids. You should be thanking me for all of the fun and joy and thrills I've given you."

Regina said, "Yeah, I thought one of you boys made this. It could have been so much better with a woman's touch."

"Yup," Kimberly said, giggling.

A broad smile stretched across Regina's face. Then the corners of her mouth began to twitch. She was proud of Kimberly's progress, but she feared the girl would once again withdraw into her shell as soon as the counselors were gone. She wasn't going to be there to hold Kimberly's hand all summer. She jogged to the front of the line.

Walking beside Kimberly, Regina said, "Told you it would be fun. You ready to start crawling?" Kimberly nodded. Regina said, "Perfect. Now, don't forget, you're the leader right now. You *have* to keep moving, okay? You don't want to hold up the line or have to start at the back again, right?"

"Don't worry, I can do this. I'm going to finish without starting over. Really."

"Love the confidence, kiddo," Regina said. She turned her attention to Christina and asked, "Are you two going to watch each other's backs?"

Kimberly and Christina looked at each other. They

giggled and nodded. Kimberly blushed as she continued walking.

"I love seeing teamwork, girls," Regina said. She stopped walking and said, "Teamwork and friendship, my two favorite words."

As he walked past Regina, his outstretched hand a few centimeters away from her face, a chubby boy said, "That's, like, four words."

"*Ha,*" Regina responded with faux amusement. "You're funny. Now go be funny somewhere else."

"I'm going to be funny in first place."

From the front of the line, Kimberly said, "Nuh-uh."

"Uh-huh!"

Regina huffed and rolled her eyes, amused by the innocent bickering. She stepped back and watched the line, allowing the other counselors to squeeze past her. She couldn't see the back of the line, but it looked like everything was under control. The counselors and campers seemed happy, so she marched forward.

But every group had at least *one* bad apple.

The campers called him a 'party pooper.' Some of the counselors called him a 'spoiler.' If Alvin had to choose one word to describe him, he would have picked '*lazy.*'

His name was Matt Reed.

Matt straggled behind the rest of the group. He fiddled with his flip phone as he plodded down the path. To his total disappointment, there was no reception in the woods, so he couldn't send text messages to his friends back home or call his girlfriend. *Tetris* and *Solitaire* were installed on the phone, but he could barely see a thing on the device's tiny monochrome display.

"Come the fuck on, man," he muttered. "Give me a bar. Give me something."

Eyes glued to the screen, he raised the phone overhead and swung it around. He took a few steps to his right, then to his left, then back to his right. The signal symbol remained the same.

No bars.

"This is such bullshit, dude," he said as if he were speaking to someone. "Cheap-ass Alvin. What the hell does he expect us to do if there's an emergency? Huh? Run out to the middle of the road and wave someone down? Shoot a flare or some shit? Who does he think we are? Instead of buying those stupid rowboats, he should have paid for a... a signal tower or something."

Matt was a lot of things—selfish, inattentive, lazy—but he wasn't really a terrible person. He had just graduated from high school and he was preparing to head out to college in the fall. He had been to Camp Blaze before as a camper, but his parents insisted on him spending one more summer there so he could learn to become more responsible by working as a counselor.

He was only lashing out because he didn't want to

be there. Most of the other counselors understood his frustration, so they didn't give him a hard time about it.

Matt sighed and closed the phone. His gaze wandered to the obstacle course. About fifteen meters ahead of him, he could see a camper—a red-haired girl —on the makeshift balance beam at the back of the line. Most of the campers had already begun crawling under the net, worming their way towards the tire pit. His fellow counselors didn't seem too concerned about his lollygagging, either.

"Whatever," he whispered. "Let's just get this–"

He stopped upon hearing a couple of heavy footsteps behind him. Then the sound of a *cracking* twig made him squinch his face up. He looked over his shoulder and immediately recoiled. From the periphery of his vision, he saw a hulking man—much taller and bigger than anyone else at the camp— standing behind him.

Before he could get a good look at him, the man swung a long plank of wood—one of the obstacle course's balance beams—at Matt's face. The cell phone fell out of his hand. The counselor's nose broke with an unnerving *crunching* sound while the plank *snapped* in half. Blood gushed out of Matt's collapsed nostrils, spilling over his lips and dripping off his chin.

Dazed by the blow, Matt wobbled in every direction until he crashed into a tree. He leaned against the trunk to regain his balance. Although he stood motionless, he felt the ground moving under him, as if he were standing in a merry-go-round. Blood dripped onto his palm as he held his hand up to his busted face. A weak *yelp* escaped his mouth as he touched the deep gash on the bridge of his nose.

He snorted while attempting to breathe through his clogged nostrils. He coughed a red haze, then he spit a blob of blood at the muddy path. Without moving away from the tree, he turned until he was leaning back against the trunk. The blow to the face left him disoriented and groggy, his thoughts scrambled and his perception warped.

He saw the sky as an ocean and the clouds as sailboats while the leaves around him smelled like they were made of copper. And he felt an earthquake, too—the most powerful earthquake ever.

It took him a moment to find his bearings.

"Wha–Wha–What ha–happened?" he stammered, head slumped forward.

The man stepped in front of him. Matt froze up. He could see his attacker's steel-toed boots and hooded coveralls. A part of him told him to run. '*Get the hell outta there!*' Another part of him told him to keep his head down. '*He'll go away if you don't make eye contact.*' The voices in his head were deafening. He took one step away from the tree, then he fell back against the trunk. He was too weak to run.

Teary-eyed, he slowly raised his head. A fresh stream of blood came out of his nose and tickled his lips. He found himself facing a man in a white mask.

He looked to his left. The path was curved, so he could no longer see the other counselors or campers beyond the trees and bushes. He heard some faint voices and laughter, though. *Scream*, he thought. *Scream and run.*

As he lurched away, he yelled, "Help! He–" Before he could take more than three steps, the masked man grabbed a fistful of his hair and pulled him back. Matt cried, "*Ow! Ow!*"

Some of Matt's hair was torn off his scalp, blonde locks sticking out from between his attacker's fingers. Blood covered the small bald spots at the back of the counselor's head.

"Stop!" Matt shouted. "Please, man, don't–"

The masked man swept his legs out from under him. Matt hit the ground hard. The wind was knocked out of him. He crossed his arms over his stomach and rocked from side to side as he struggled to draw a decent breath. Oxygen came into his lungs in short, painful rasps.

The killer picked up the cell phone. He flipped it open, read the display—*still no bars*—then shut it. He shoved the phone into the counselor's mouth. Matt closed his eyes tightly as the device hit the back of his throat. His tongue slithered out of his mouth from under the phone, the tip quivering like a snake's.

The killer punted Matt's chin like a football. The *thud* echoed through the forest. A sluggish, ghastly groan came out of Matt's mouth.

At the back of the line, the redheaded girl peeked

over her shoulder. She didn't see anyone, but she believed one of the monsters from Kenneth's stories was following them.

Bigfoot, she thought, eyes wide with horror.

She jumped off the last balance beam, then dropped to her stomach and started crawling under the net. She moved so quickly out of fear that she pulled herself out of last place.

Matt's stiff arms shot up, forearms extended into the air. Some of his fingers were curled halfway while the others stuck out in all directions. His teeth cut into the underside of his tongue, nearly severing it. And his teeth kept grinding while he fought to stay conscious. He was unintentionally *sawing* into his tongue. The phone's display cracked and the battery cover broke in his mouth.

Frothy saliva mixed with blood spumed out of his mouth. The red goops slid down his cheeks. A mass of the bubbly blood blocked his right ear.

The killer grabbed another fistful of Matt's hair and dragged him away from the obstacle course. Matt wanted to scream and fight, but he felt like he had lost complete control of his body. His vocal cords were out of order and his arms were disobedient. Twigs hit his shoulders and leaves brushed his face as he was pulled through a bush.

They were hidden amongst the trees and foliage, although some rays of sunshine penetrated the branches above them. They could no longer hear the other counselors or campers, either.

The killer crouched behind Matt and put him in a rear naked choke. He used enough pressure to smother his voice and restrain him, but not enough to suffocate him. The broken phone rode a slimy wave of blood out of Matt's mouth as he gasped for air.

Through his blurred, pulsing vision, Matt watched as the killer extended his free hand in front of them. He was holding a multitool. He withdrew his hand, then extended it again. A serrated three-inch blade stuck out of the multitool. The man waggled the knife at Matt, as if to say: '*No, not this.*' He withdrew his hand for a moment, then extended it once more. He showed the counselor the multitool's wire cutter component. He shook the tool at him again.

'*No, not that one, either.*'

He pulled his arm back. Matt could hear him tinkering with the multitool, but he couldn't see it. He felt his heartbeat accelerating as the possibilities raced through his mind. *He's going to use the knife,* he thought, silent tears coursing down his bloody cheeks. *No, the wire cutter. No, a screwdriver. He's going to kill me. I'm dead, I'm dead, I'm dead.* His eyes grew as the man's hand emerged in his vision again. He was surprised to see the multitool's bottle opener.

"Wa–Wa–Wait," he croaked out, his voice barely louder than the breeze.

In a hushed voice, so soft that it was impossible to identify, the killer said, "See no evil."

He thrust the bottle opener at Matt's left eye. Matt tried to scream, but only a throaty gasp came out. The bottle opener's tooth pierced his eye. The killer wiggled it around until the fulcrum slid under the counselor's upper eyelid. The tooth sank deeper into his eyeball. A mixture of blood, tears, and vitreous rimmed his eyelids.

The killer moved the multitool up and down like a lever. Matt's eye jutted out. The muscles attached to his eye tore with a *crackling* sound, like autumn leaves crumbling under a person's shoes. But his eye was too big for the bottle opener's ring. As the killer pushed the handle down, Matt's eye was nearly cut in half vertically. The front half flew up, his pupil looking at the tree branches above them.

A gelatinous fluid poured out of his eye's exposed vitreous center. Strings of slimy blood hung over his cheek.

Matt's gasping turned into groaning. And, as the pain zapped through his skull like a bullet, his groaning grew into a bellow.

The killer tightened his grip on the counselor's neck, but he couldn't stifle his crying. He drew the serrated blade from the multitool and held it in the icepick grip. He released Matt from the rear naked choke. Before the counselor even realized it, the masked man stabbed him in the neck. It looked like an

MMA fighter throwing hammerfists at his opponent's throat.

Blood spritzed out of the first three stab wounds like small sprays of cologne, dripping onto the counselor's shoulders and the mud below him. Then the blood burst out as his jugular was punctured with the fourth stab. But the killer didn't stop. He stabbed the side of Matt's neck thirteen times. Matt passed away less than a minute after the brutal attack. The blood from his butchered neck soaked the upper half of his shirt. It looked black in the shadows.

The masked killer rolled the teenager's corpse under a set of bushes. It wasn't the best hiding place, but it was good enough. Drops of blood stained his gloves, sleeves, and mask, but he didn't seem to mind. He returned to the path and checked the obstacle course. There was no one in sight, but he heard the faint echoes of happiness to his left. He walked in the opposite direction, casually fleeing the murder scene in broad daylight.

A SMILE OF RELIEF BLOSSOMED ON REGINA'S FACE AS they reached the main campsite. She spun in place to face the line of tired campers—mud caked on their elbows and knees, faces blazing red, sweat dripping from everywhere. They were all smiling and giggling, though. The counselors fared much better. She could see Oscar and Kenneth had hardly broken a sweat. They didn't have to crawl, hop, or climb after all.

Regina caught everyone's attention with a loud clap. She said, "Listen up, ladies and gentlemen. If you're dirty, I want you to hit the showers and change your clothes. Now, I know some of you are very, *very* lazy, so if you won't take a shower, at least scrub your-selves down at the sinks and fountains. But *not* the drinking fountains, okay?" The campers chatted amongst themselves. Regina said, "C'mon, what are you waiting for? You want to look good, don't you?"

Some of the girls answered with a synchronized: "*Yes!*"

Over a few groans and mutters, the boys answered with '*noes,*' '*nopes,*' and '*nahs.*'

"Well, for those of you who said no, it doesn't matter. Clean yourselves up, boys and girls, or I'll throw you in the lake at night while you're sleeping," Regina said, half-jokingly. While some of the kids laughed and scoffed at her playful threat, the counselor said, "After you're cleaned up—and, again, you *will* be cleaned up—you'll have a couple of options. You can either do arts and crafts in the quad or head out to the archery range."

Oscar said, "Kenny and I will also be at the basketball courts and I think some of the ladies will be playing beach volleyball. You can come hang out with any of us, too."

"Sure, that's fine, too. *But* you can't go into the water. Understand? I'm serious about this."

Kimberly stood in front of her peers, hands on her hips as she caught her breath. She finished the obstacle course in fourth place. It was good enough for her. Her happiness quickly turned into confusion—and confusion into curiosity. She squinted an eye and tilted her head to the side. The campers had been allowed to swim in the lake all summer. They weren't allowed to board the rowboats without a counselor's supervision, but they were free to swim near the shore as much as they pleased. As someone who enjoyed the camp's water activities, the sudden change in rules struck her as odd.

She raised her hand and asked, "Why not?"

Most of the campers and counselors looked at the girl. No one expected her to speak out. Some of them had never even heard her voice.

Regina said, "It's just for today, Kim. We had a... a little mix up with the schedule, so we don't have enough counselors to take care of you while you swim. We're a little too busy with the arts and crafts and the archery and the... the basketball and all that good stuff. So, please, everyone, just stay out of the water for now."

Regina gave Kimberly a half-hearted smile, as if to say: '*Sorry, hope you understand.*' The kids started gossiping, buzzing like a hornet's nest.

A chubby boy said, "It's because there's so much pee in the water."

"Gross," a girl responded.

In a matter-of-fact tone, another boy said, "I pee in there every day."

Regina wanted to tell them about Taylor and Carol, but she didn't want to alarm them. She couldn't afford to lose control of the situation. *Lie to them,* she told herself. *Tell them that it is pee. Tell 'em something, anything.* She didn't feel comfortable lying to them. She didn't want to arouse the other counselors' suspicion, either. She assumed most of them knew the truth, so lies would only complicate their relationships. As the head counselor, she couldn't lose their trust.

"Regina!" a male voice echoed through the campsite.

She looked over her shoulder and spotted Alvin near the quad. She held her pointer finger up—'One second, please!'

She faced the campers and said, "Just trust me, okay? Everything will be back to normal soon. I'll be at the archery range after I talk to Mr. Perry. Have fun, all of you."

"Bye!" Kimberly shouted as she stumbled forward.

Walking backwards, Regina winked and said, "See you soon."

She smiled and waved at the campers, trying to keep a semblance of control. She approached Alvin as the group dispersed behind her. Before she could say a word, Alvin beckoned to her and walked away. She followed him around the corner to the other side of the cafeteria. Her lips drooped into a frown upon spotting the police presence.

Officers Dominic Marino and Ian Miller were waiting behind the cafeteria. They were dressed in matching tan uniforms. Based on his aura of command, Regina could see Marino was in charge of the investigation. His black hair was combed over, a few wavy strands hanging over his brow, and stubble covered his jaw. He held a small notepad and pen in his hands, ready to take notes like an eager college student.

Miller hung back a little, quiet but attentive. He was there to assist Marino—to help him catch the little details.

Regina said, "You know, if you really want this to be 'discreet,' we should probably do this somewhere a bit more private. The kids are going to be in the quad soon."

"We won't take much of your time," Marino said in a strong but pleasant voice.

Regina crossed her arms, shook her head, and said, "Fine. How can I help you?"

"Well, ma'am, according to Mr. Perry here, two of your coworkers have gone missing. We've been told you'd be able to tell us more about the situation."

"Just tell them what you told me, dear," Alvin said.

Regina said, "Well, um... Last night, Taylor and Carol left the–"

"Full names, please," Marino interrupted.

"*Taylor Harris* and *Carol Chambers* left the campsite to go 'mess around.' They're a couple and they wanted some time alone. I figured it wasn't a big deal. When we were returning from the campfire an hour or two before midnight, Mr. Perry told me that he couldn't get ahold of Taylor. We thought they would be back by the morning, but we haven't seen either of them all day."

"Taylor and Carol, they're over eighteen years old, correct? They're adults?"

"Yes."

Marino nodded as he scribbled on his notepad. From Regina's angle, his writing was illegible, like gang graffiti on rubble.

Marino asked, "Can you describe them for me? The more detail, the better. Tattoos, birthmarks, hair color, height, weight, it all helps."

Regina sighed, then she said, "Jeez, I don't know. They look like... like normal people. Young adults, y'know? Carol's hair is black and curly. Taylor's hair is short and black. Carol is... a little shorter than me and Taylor's probably a foot taller. They don't have any tattoos. I mean, I've never seen any on them and I've —*unfortunately*—seen them both naked." She glanced at Alvin and asked, "Don't you have their pictures in the administration building?"

"We do," Alvin responded. "Every counselor has a– a file with their picture, contact information, and contract in my office. I told these gentlemen all about it already."

Marino said, "You did. And we'll get that from you soon. But we'll need more than headshots if we're going to find these kids." He jotted another note down, then he said, "So, they departed before you reached the campfire. Where did they go?"

Regina pointed to her right and said, "They got off on that path. Past those cabins right there. It's like I told Mr. Perry: They could have gone to the old tool-shed, the boathouse, or the shore. I guess they could have even left the camp, but I really don't know if they'd do something like that."

"Who was the last person to see them?"

Regina shrugged and said, "I guess that would be... me and Oscar."

"Oscar?"

"Oscar Orozco. He's another counselor here."

Although his writing was sloppy, Regina could see Marino had written Oscar's name on his notepad.

She said, "I don't think any of us did anything wrong, sir. They just wanted to have a romantic night. That's all."

Marino kept writing while Miller studied Regina's demeanor. She started fidgeting. She felt like the prime suspect in a murder case.

Looking over his notes, Marino said, "Great. I'm just going to need the emergency contact information for Mr. Harris and Ms. Chambers. We'll have to inform their guardians about the situation if you haven't done so already."

Alvin said, "I think that's a good idea."

Marino took a step closer to Regina and said, "For the time being, I want you to stay out of the forest. No late-night excursions, no campfires in the woods, no camping in tents. You stay on campgrounds and you sleep in your cabins. And that goes for both campers *and* counselors. I'd also like all of you to stay away from the toolshed and boathouse. After we call their parents, my partner and I are going to do a brief walk through of those areas, then we'll be out of your hair."

Marino's statement made Regina uneasy. '*We'll be out of your hair.*' The cops seemed observant and methodical, but they didn't inspire much hope.

"But what if you don't find them?" Regina asked. "What? You're just... You're going to give up? Leave and pretend like everything's okay?"

Marino explained, "We're conducting a *formal* investigation, ma'am. We're going to use all available resources, but we can't bring out the hounds just yet. At the moment, we have no idea if these counselors are injured or if there was any foul play involved in their disappearances. For all we know, this young couple could have run off, eloped, and rented a hotel room in town. They're adults, not children." He nodded at Alvin—'*Lead the way.*' As the group walked away, he said, "Thank you for your assistance. We'll keep you updated."

Regina could only stay behind and watch as her boss led the police to the administration building. She heard the happy campers yelling and laughing on the other side of the cafeteria, but she felt nothing but anger, fear, and disappointment. She dropped her arms to her sides and took a few deep breaths, then she forced an uncertain smile onto her face.

"Act normal," she whispered as she headed to the archery range. "They're going to find them. They *have* to find them."

Arrows soared across the field. A few struck the foam targets at the end while most hit the surrounding lawn. The projectiles sang a song of *whooshing* and *thudding* with each shot. The gentle breeze blew some of the arrows into the woods. That small square area beyond the targets was gated and restricted during the activity to prevent accidents.

Regina walked back and forth behind the line of archers, like a supervisor at a sweatshop. She occasionally offered tips for better accuracy and warned about the dangers of misusing a compound bow. She appeared distant, though. Thoughts of tragedy infected her mind with sorrow. She was beginning to grieve without any confirmed deaths.

She stopped and gazed at the child at the end of the line—*Kimberly*.

The kid was skilled at archery. With her steady

hands and proper posture, she hit the targets with ease. The compound bow and the release aid certainly helped her out, but her talent was undeniable. As a matter of fact, she was responsible for all of the bullseyes at the range during that sunny noontime.

Regina approached her and said, "Woah, kiddo, you're really good at this. I'm seriously impressed. I used to shoot a little, too, but I was *never* as good as you. Who taught you?"

Kimberly lowered the bow and shrugged. She said, "I've had a bunch of teachers. My dad used to teach me, but he's been super busy for, um... for a long time. Like, busy for a lot of years, y'know?"

"I'm sure he wants to spend more time with you, sweetie, but he's just... just..."

"Just too busy?" Kimberly asked, pouting.

Regina knelt in front of her and said, "Yeah. My dad was like that, too. I didn't really understand it until I was older. Now, I know he was busy because he cared about me, about our family. He needed to work to support us, even if it meant spending less time with us. I'm sure your father is working hard to support you. I know it, Kimberly. You know he cares about you, right?"

"I know. He tells me that a lot. And he sends me to camp because he wants me to have fun," Kimberly said. She looked at the field, watching as arrows soared through the sky like a flock of birds. Staring at the targets, she asked, "Can you shoot a bullseye?"

"No, no, no. I can probably hit a target, but I can't shoot a bullseye. I usually practice archery when I have a lot on my mind. It helps me focus and... and relieve stress. It really helped me get through high school and it even helps a little in college. I don't get to do it much anymore, so I'm a little rusty."

Kimberly looked down. Thoughts of school made her anxiety surge. She enjoyed studying, her grades were great, but she feared socializing. She had nightmares of giving in-class presentations. She was interested in college, though. Her parents had told her that it was a completely different experience.

She asked, "Regina, what's college like?"

'*I usually study until dawn, and I sometimes smoke weed, go out and drink, and party with my friends.*' Regina bit her lower lip to stop herself from telling Kimberly the complete truth. She wasn't ashamed of her behavior—it wasn't like she was going out of her way to hurt people—she just didn't want to set a bad example.

She said, "Well, it's a whole lot easier than high school, sweetie. The homework and tests might be a little harder, but everything else is easier. You get to make your own schedule, you can meet people who share common interests, and most professors won't make you do stupid presentations." She noticed the smile of relief pulling on Kimberly's lips. She patted the girl's shoulder and said, "Trust me, Kim, it gets easier. A girl like yourself will do just fine."

"Thank you," Kimberly said.

"*Boo!*" Oscar yelled.

Regina and Kimberly flinched and gasped. They hadn't noticed him creeping up on them. Regina got up to her feet and shoved him gently while Kimberly giggled.

Oscar asked, "What were you girls talking about over here? *Me?*"

"Eww," Kimberly groaned playfully. "Why would we be talking about you?"

"Why *wouldn't* you be talking about me? Right, Regina? I'm good-looking, I'm sweet, I'm–"

"Okay, okay," Regina interrupted. "Enough bragging, hotshot. What do you want?"

"Came to see if you wanted to grab a bite to eat."

"Now?"

"Yeah, *now*," Oscar responded with a big nod. "Kimberly can come with us. Chase and Michael can clean up, right?"

Regina looked at the field. The lawn and woods were strewn with arrows. She felt bad about leaving the mess for the other counselors. She saw the excitement and hope in Kimberly's eyes, though. The girl wanted to join them.

"Fine," Regina said. She rubbed Kimberly's shoulder and said, "Let's put your bow away, then grab something to eat. I'm sure Chase won't mind cleaning up anyway. Besides, if he complains, we'll just fire him."

"Can I do it?" Kimberly asked.

The group chatted and laughed as they departed from the archery range.

"You've gotta be kidding me," Chase Fletcher said as he removed his green baseball cap.

He leaned away from the lamppost and pressed the back of his hand against his sweaty forehead. Squinting, he looked past the targets and into the woods. A camper's arrow flew over the gated zone and landed somewhere in the forest. The archer, a tubby eleven-year-old boy named Joey, snickered while sharing high fives with his buddies.

Chase looked at him and said, "You did that on purpose, didn't you?"

"It was an accident," Joey said through his gritted teeth as he tried to stop himself from laughing.

"You think it's funny?"

"N–No, it's... My bad."

Joey covered his mouth and chuckled. His pals laughed, too. Chase dug his fingers into his curly brown hair and sighed. He was so angry that he started laughing with them.

He said, "I'm going to have to go out there and find that damn arrow. You know that, right?"

"Why? Just leave it out there. We won't tell anyone."

"If I leave it out there, one of you kids might trip

and smash your heads on a tree or poke your eye out if you find that arrow. We don't want that. Or do we?"

"No one's going to fall out there. No one ever falls, dude."

"Is that so? Why don't we both go out there and you can–"

"Listen up!" Chelsea Martinez shouted, standing behind the line of amateur archers. "It's time to head back to the quad. I'd really appreciate it if you kids wrote a short letter to your parents. I don't want them worrying about you. C'mon, c'mon. Put your bows away. Chase will clean everything else up. Right, Chase?"

Chase smiled wearily and nodded—'*Sure, whatever*.' No one wanted to be assigned cleanup duty at Camp Blaze. But he agreed to it in order to get on Chelsea's good side. At twenty years old, one year older than him, Chelsea was a raven-haired young woman with a kind heart and a curvy body. He was attracted to her like ants to sugar. He had been trying all summer to get 'something' going with her. And she had finally agreed to meet him later that night for a private chat.

Chelsea said, "Great. Come on, kids. Follow me."

"Ah, shit," Chase muttered, eyes glued to her ass. "I should have said something funny. Should have said... *anything*. I hope she doesn't cancel on me."

He stuck around and supervised the campers as they put their bows away. He didn't lock up the supplies, though. He didn't want to lock and unlock the supply shed over and over. He figured he would save time by finding Joey's arrow first so he wouldn't have to carry all of the projectiles into the woods with him or make multiple trips across the archery range.

He carefully traversed the woods, lunging over the puddles of mud to avoid dirtying his white sneakers. He got mud on them anyway.

"That tub of lard is going to clean my fuckin' shoes after this, I swear to God," he muttered.

He kept his head low and searched for the arrow. To his utter disappointment, the arrow had a light brown shaft, so it blended with the environment. The dirt, mud, twigs, branches, and trunks, they were all different shades of the same color—*brown*. He picked up a couple of twigs, kicked a few stones, and pushed some bushes, but he couldn't find the arrow.

"I should have dragged that brat out here and made *him* find it," he said. "I'm stuck out here looking for a damn arrow while he's writing to mommy and daddy. Such bullshit. I'm gonna make him–"

He heard a quiet voice behind him. His face tightened while a rash of goosebumps spread across his limbs. He turned around. There was no one there. He cut his eyes up to the tree branches above him. The branches looked like they were waving at him thanks to the wind. He didn't see anyone in the trees, though.

He huffed, then he said, "If you're trying to mess with me, kid, I swear I'm going to make you pay. And I don't care if you run to Regina or Alvin. I'm gonna pull your crap-stained underwear over your head, then give you the longest swirlie of your life. You hear me?" There was no answer. He sneered and whispered, "Little punk."

From somewhere behind him, a soft voice called out: "Over here."

Chase's muscles contracted and a tingly sensation shot up his spine. He turned around again, completing a 360-degree turn. He spotted a few rustling bushes. He didn't see anyone out there, but he felt like someone was watching him. He staggered back and searched for a weapon—a branch, a stone, *anything*.

"Joey, I'm going to kick your ass, you... you little bitch," he said with a hint of doubt in his voice. "Kenneth! Kenny, if that's you, you asshole, I'm going to sock you, man!"

"Ash remembers what you did," the soft voice said.

"Huh?"

"Ash never forgets."

"A–Ash?"

A gust of wind blew through the area. His ears were attacked by the loudest swishing, crackling, and groaning he had ever heard at the campsite. He turned and lurched away, but he slid to a sudden stop after six wobbly steps. Time slowed to a crawl. He felt every heartbeat in his chest, every large bead of cold sweat sliding down his face, and every hair at the nape of his neck sway.

A tall person in navy coveralls and a ghostly mask

stood near the gated zone some thirty meters away. He held a compound bow with an arrow nocked and the bowstring drawn.

Chase felt a scream surging up his throat, but he didn't have the opportunity to yell. Time resumed at its regular pace with the *snap* of the bow as the masked man shot the arrow. Eyes big and mouth gaping, one thought rattled around in Chase's head: *This can't be happening*. Then he squeezed his eyes shut, gagged, and teetered back as the arrow hit his neck.

It penetrated the center of his throat, impaling his windpipe and esophagus. It hit his spine with enough force to fracture some of his cervical vertebrae, then slid around it and stuck out from the back of his neck. A piece of his Adam's apple—bloody cartilage— seeped out from the exit wound. He could see the arrow's fletching under his chin and hear his blood dripping from the arrowhead behind him.

He took a couple of heavy, unsteady steps back. His lips moved, but only croaks and groans came out of his mouth. He crashed into a tree behind him.

"Ash never forgets," the mysterious voice repeated.

It didn't sound like it was coming from the man in front of him, though. He felt like it was coming to him from everywhere—the trees, the ground, *his own head*. His masked attacker approached him. He stopped about twenty meters away, nocked another arrow, drew the bowstring, then aimed it at Chase. The counselor raised a trembling hand at him, begging for mercy without saying a word.

The masked man shot the arrow.

The projectile skewered Chase's palm and sent his hand flying back towards his face, causing the counselor to backhand himself. The arrowhead punctured his eye, broke his eye socket, and came to a stop halfway into his brain. Hand fastened to his face, he slid down to his ass, then fell to his side. His head landed under a bush next to Joey's arrow.

The masked archer stood there and watched him, analyzing every twitch and listening to every moan. He waited until Chase stopped moving—about a minute —then he departed.

7

REGINA STROLLED DOWN THE PATH, HANDS IN HER windbreaker's pockets. The camp was at its coolest and calmest at night.

As she approached three boys standing near the bathroom, Regina asked, "What are you little guys doing out here? You wouldn't be trying to peek into the girls' bathroom, would you?"

Kyle, a twelve-year-old boy with bushy black hair, shook his head and stuttered, "N–No, we–we... We're just, um... We..."

"You were just going to your cabins, *right?*"

"Um, ye–yeah. Yeah, that's right."

"Good. If you have to pee, go ahead and do it now. I don't want to see you out here when I come back, though. I better not catch you peeping, either. I'm serious, okay?"

Kyle said, "We won't."

"We promise," another boy said.

Regina said, "Well, go on and finish your business. You're going to catch a cold standing out here without your sweaters."

She patted Kyle's head as she walked past him and continued her nightly patrol. She kept a small smile on her face to keep up appearances, but she couldn't hide the distant look in her eyes. She couldn't stop thinking about the missing counselors.

She spotted Kenneth with a new junior counselor, Jennifer Rhodes. Jennifer leaned back against a lamp-post, twirling her hair and snickering childishly. They didn't have much in common, but they were attracted to each other.

Regina shouted, "Jenny! I'd be careful around him if I were you! I saw him spending some 'quality time' with a tree last night, who knows what else he'd stick it in!"

Jennifer held her hand over her mouth and blushed. Kenneth wasn't amused. *Cock-blocker,* he thought.

He said, "I wouldn't be talking, Regina. I thought I saw Oscar with that same tree a few nights ago."

"Oh really?" Regina asked. "So, you like his sloppy seconds or something?"

"Why are you asking? You interested in something?"

"See? Told you, Jen, he'd stick it in anything. Be careful around this guy."

Smiling awkwardly, Jennifer responded, "I think I can handle him."

"You think so?" Kenneth said, smirking.

As she walked past them, Regina said, "You 'kids' have a good night and stay out of the woods, okay?"

She kept walking until she reached the Gators cabins. She found Chelsea standing near a portable toilet. One after the other, her knees moved to and fro. Her brow was creased and her teeth sank into her bottom lip. Regina could tell something was bothering her.

She asked, "What's up, Chelsea? Are you, um... You waiting for Chase?" Chelsea nodded. Regina asked, "Everything okay between you two?"

Chelsea said, "Oh yeah, we're good. We've been talking a lot more recently and stuff, but... I haven't seen him for a few hours. I left him at the archery range. He was supposed to clean up, then we... we, um..." She stepped closer to Regina and, in a quiet voice but louder than a whisper, she said, "We were supposed to meet at the quad after arts and crafts, but he never showed up."

Regina started to tremble like a wet chihuahua. *A third disappearance?* she thought. She stared down the path behind her and tried to recollect every detail of her patrol. She couldn't remember seeing Chase.

She said, "He's probably with the boys. I'm sure he'll show up. Don't... Don't worry about it too much."

Chelsea sighed, then she said, "Yeah, you're probably right. It's just that he's usually not like that. He's 'one of the boys,' sure, but he's always been a... I don't know, maybe it sounds silly, but he's always been a gentleman to me. When we agree to do something, he honors it."

"I get it. I'll let you know if I see him. If I had to guess, Alvin probably asked him to help him in the kitchen or with the rowboats."

"I could forgive him if Alvin had something to do with it, but... Regina, I just have a bad feeling in my stomach. Something's not right."

'*Me too*.' Regina stopped herself from saying those words aloud.

She grunted, then she said, "I'm going to talk to Oscar. If anyone knows anything, it'll be him. I'll be back at the counselors' cabin when I'm finished with my rounds. I'll see you there, right?"

Chelsea just nodded.

Regina hurried away. She swung her head frantically as she searched for Oscar. She stopped upon hearing his voice. She glanced to her right and saw him leaving the Gators' cabin.

Walking backwards, he hollered, "Good night! Don't let the–"

Regina grabbed his arm and pulled him away. He nearly lost his footing as he followed her into the woods. She stopped behind a tree. They were hidden in the shadows, but they could see the bright cabins and illuminated pathways from their position.

Oscar said, "Woah. Now what are we going to do out–"

"We have to talk," Regina interrupted.

Oscar said, "Talk? This seems like a strange place to talk, doesn't it? Unless we're going to talk about, you know, foolin' around. Are we..." A grin stretched across his face. He asked, "Are we about to fool around?"

"I'm serious, Oscar. Chase is... I think he's missing."

"Chase is missing? No, that doesn't sound right. He's around here somewhere. Probably screwing around with Kenneth or something."

"I just saw Kenneth with Jennifer. He wasn't with them. Chelsea hasn't seen him all afternoon, either. Did you see him after we left the archery range?"

Oscar inhaled deeply through his nose and looked at the surrounding cabins. He considered lying to Regina to calm her nerves. He didn't want to jeopardize Chase's safety if he was actually missing, though.

"No, I haven't seen him," he said. "But—*but*—he has to be around here somewhere. People don't just disappear without a trace."

"*Exactly,*" Regina responded, her eyes bugging out. "Maybe it wouldn't be a big deal if we haven't seen him, but Chelsea? Everyone knows they've been crushing hard on each other. If anyone knows where he's at, she does—*and she doesn't*. Something's wrong."

"Don't go jumping to conclusions. That never ends well. Are you sure you've checked everywhere and asked everyone?"

"I can't go out there and interrogate everyone. I... I can't cause a scene. But I've made my rounds and I didn't see him. Where are you coming from?"

Oscar said, "I was at the counselors' cabin for a while, then I came over here."

"Did you see him at the counselors' cabin? Was he there?"

Oscar shook his head.

Regina said, "We have to tell Alvin about this."

"Are you sure you're not overreacting? The guy could be in the woods taking a piss or smoking a joint."

"He could be doing a lot of things, but we're not going into the woods to look for him now. It's too dark, too dangerous. Listen, Taylor and Carol never showed up, either. Something is seriously wrong. We have to tell Alvin. We need the police. Come with me. *Please*."

Oscar saw the fear in her eyes and regret on her shoulders. She was responsible for their safety. With the disappearances piling up, she felt like she was failing them.

Oscar said, "Fine. Let's just hope he's still in his office."

"Let's hurry," Regina said as she grabbed his hand.

Regina and Oscar sat across from Alvin, chairs creaking under their weight. A big, sturdy desk sat between the owner and the counselors. The walls were decorated with photographs of the camp's yearly visitors. The pictures dated back to 1989.

Alvin lowered his glasses to the tip of his nose and inspected his visitor. Regina couldn't sit still as she bit her fingernails while Oscar stayed calm and quiet.

"I was just about to make my last phone call of the night before you two barged in here," Alvin said. "How may I help you?"

Regina rubbed her temple and said, "I can't take this anymore, sir. I'm getting... *paranoid*. There, I said it. If you think I'm going crazy and you want to send me home, then you do what you have to do. But that's the truth. Taylor and Carol haven't shown up yet and now Chase, another counselor, has gone missing."

"Excuse me?"

"Chase Fletcher is missing, Mr. Perry."

Alvin leaned back in his seat, stunned by the development. He grumbled indistinctly to himself, then he took off his glasses and put his elbows on the table, fingers interlocked under his chin.

He asked, "And your positive about this?"

Regina said, "I can't give you a 100-percent guarantee, but I *can* say that I haven't seen him, Oscar hasn't seen him, and neither has Chelsea. I called out to him on the radio before we came in here and he didn't answer."

"I see."

There was a moment of silence.

"That's it?" Regina asked, growing agitated.

"Alvin... Mr. Perry, sir, what are we going to do? Please tell me you realize this is a very serious situation."

"I do, Regina, I do," Alvin said. "I'm just dealing with a lot. You see, before you two came in here, I was just about to call the police once again."

"Why?" Oscar asked.

"I was approached by another counselor earlier this evening. I believe it was Ms. Angela Grant. She asked me a peculiar question. She asked... She asked if I had finally sent Matt Reed home. And she asked this because that boy was always playing on his phone and slacking off, leaving his duties for the others. And... Well, she hadn't seen him all day."

Regina stuttered, "A–Are you saying Matt is also missing?"

"It would seem so, yes," Alvin said with disappointment in his voice.

Regina sank into her seat and stared vacantly at his desk. Oscar looked at the window to his right and thought about the possibilities. There was a sudden sense of real danger.

Alvin said, "Give me a minute. I'm going to call Officer Marino and see if we can get him out here." He stood from his seat. As he walked past the counselors, he said, "I'd like to do this in private."

The counselors didn't move until they heard the door close behind them.

Regina said, "I told you something was going on.

That's *four* missing counselors, Oscar. Four of our friends. God, what do you think happened to them?"

"You were right, but... I don't know. I can't really think of anything. Maybe... Maybe they fell in the woods."

"Fell in the woods? Are you kidding me?"

"I mean, what if there's a massive sinkhole out there? You've seen 'em on the news, right? Those things can be *huge*. So, what if Taylor and Carol fell into a sinkhole like that? Then maybe Matt found them and tried to help them up, but he fell, too. The same thing might have happened to Chase. They could all be stuck somewhere. I know it's not the most realistic thing or whatever, but... Listen, I just don't want your imagination to run wild."

Oscar's theory sounded absurd to Regina. *They would have been screaming for help and someone would have heard them*, she thought. She suspected foul play, and she feared one of the counselors may have been responsible.

She asked, "What if someone hurt them?"

"That's what I'm talking about, Regina. I don't want you to think like that."

"But it's possible, isn't it?"

Oscar said, "If someone hurt them, the police will get to the bottom of it."

Regina asked, "And what if they're too late?"

"Too late for–"

The door swung open. The counselors became

quiet as Alvin returned to his seat.

The owner said, "They'll be here in an hour. I couldn't get ahold of Officer Marino, so I'm not sure who they're sending, but they're sending someone."

"Good," Regina said.

She was worried about her peers and the campers. The imminent police presence brought some comfort to her mind.

Alvin said, "Now for some bad news. I'm thinking about closing the camp early if our missing counselors don't show up soon. Refunds don't matter to me and you'll still be paid for your work. I just can't risk your safety or the safety of those precious kids out there. I'll ask the police for their recommendation, too, but it seems very likely that they'll agree with me."

Oscar shrugged and said, "Whatever you think is best, Mr. Perry."

"If they don't show up, we'll close Camp Blaze by the end of the upcoming weekend. How does that sound?"

Oscar nodded at him. Regina was lost in her thoughts. Paychecks weren't important to her. The camp's security was her primary concern. She agreed with Alvin's plan to close the camp, but she disagreed with the timing. Sunday was five days away. She thought of it as five days with a target on her back.

"How does that sound?" Alvin repeated, eyes on Regina.

Regina looked at the ceiling to prevent her tears

from falling. She said, "It's fine."

"Excellent. I sincerely hope it doesn't come to that. I wish this was all one sick prank. Still, I want you to stay vigilant. You never know. So, I would really appreciate it if you did a few more rounds tonight. Maybe—and I know I'm asking for a lot—maybe you can wake up every two or so hours to check on the campers. It's more than what we agreed to, but it would mean a lot to me."

Oscar said, "Regina is supervising our Swim Day tomorrow, so I think she should get to bed soon. I'll do a few more rounds and check up on the cabins throughout the night."

Regina asked, "With everything that's going on, do you still want us to let the kids swim? Are you sure that's a good idea?"

Alvin responded, "I don't see a problem with it so long as you have enough lifeguards on duty. I think it's safer out on the water than in the woods, too. And I'd like those kids to enjoy the lake one more time before we close—*if* we close, that is."

Regina and Oscar nodded in agreement, then they looked at each other. Regina was terrified while Oscar was confident. Oscar grabbed her hand and gave it a gentle squeeze. Regina felt like he was transferring his confidence into her. His touch helped her relax. She drew a deep breath and nodded again.

Alvin said, "Then it's settled. You kids get some rest. I'll stay and wait for the police."

8

ROW YOUR BOAT

THE SCREAMS REVERBERATED ACROSS THE LAKE—LOUD, ceaseless, *joyful*. The campers yelled and giggled as they splashed in the water. The young swimmers wore neon swimsuits so the counselors could keep an eye on them at all times. A few kids sat on the docks and kicked their feet over the water, enjoying the warm sunshine while gossiping. A few of the campers played beach volleyball at the shore. The older kids were allowed to join the counselors on the rowboats for trips from one side of the lake to the other.

Regina and Kimberly sat in a rowboat, paddling their way across the lake at a leisurely pace. Kimberly stopped paddling to adjust the pink one-piece swimsuit she wore under her orange life jacket. Although she was still dressed in her camp uniform—a green t-shirt and matching shorts—Regina wore a life jacket, too.

"You okay?" Regina asked. "Is it too tight?"

"Just a little, but it's okay. Can we stop here?"

"You tired?"

"Not really," Kimberly said. "I just don't want to finish too fast. Is that okay?"

Regina shrugged and said, "Sure. I don't want to finish too fast, either. I'd rather just... *float away* from all of this."

Kimberly narrowed an eye and asked, "Why?"

Regina wanted to say something like: '*My friends are missing. I'm scared of this place. I want to leave as soon as possible.*' She bit her tongue, though. She didn't want to put her burden on Kimberly's fragile shoulders. The kid couldn't solve her problems anyway.

"Don't worry about it, Kim," Regina said. "Why don't you, um... Tell me about yourself, sweetie. Help me get my mind off things."

Kimberly said, "I don't know what to say. I'm kinda boring."

"You're not boring. C'mon, what do you like? What are Kimberly Morgan's hobbies?"

Kimberly's gaze shifted to the sky. She said, "Well, I like reading and I like movies. Mostly fantasy and sci-fi stuff. Um... I don't have a bunch of friends. My mom and dad are always working and my big sister is always busy with her own friends. It's lonely at home, but... I like it out here. And I like talking to you. I think you're like... like a big sister, too."

A bittersweet smile came to Regina's face. She was

happy about her positive influence but saddened by Kimberly's loneliness. She saw a shade of herself in the girl's glum eyes.

She said, "I was a lot like you, Kim. My parents were workaholics, my brothers and sisters were always busy with their friends and schoolwork, and I always felt left out. It took a while, but I was able to break out of my shell eventually. You just have to... to let yourself grow. Does that make sense?"

"Kinda."

"Try new things, take some risks, but don't ever change yourself for anyone unless that's what *you* want. Live your life the way you want to live. There's no such thing as a–a... a mind reader, y'know? So, stop thinking about what other people *might* be thinking about. It's a waste of time."

"I know," Kimberly said as she lowered her head. "It's just... Sometimes, I feel like my brain is in a washing machine. I know I shouldn't, but I keep thinking the same thoughts. It's usually stuff like... like about not wanting to make mistakes or embarrassing myself. I don't know, really. It's just really hard to explain."

Regina smiled, patted the girl's shoulder, and said, "I get it. Trust me, kiddo, you're not the only one with your brain in a washing machine. Everyone overthinks. It's part of being human. You're going to be okay, I promise. Listen, before camp ends, I'll make sure to give you my personal phone number. We can keep in touch and you can call me whenever you need advice. Does that sound good?"

Kimberly felt the sincerity—*the kindness*—in Regina's voice. Their connection grew stronger with each passing day.

She said, "Thank you, Regina."

Regina winked, then she said, "No problem, sweetie. It's my pleasure to... to be there for you and the other kids. I wouldn't be here if I didn't care about all of you. So, seriously, if you ever need anything—anything at all—I'm always right around the corner."

Kimberly didn't realize she was blushing until she saw her reflection on the lake. She reached over the edge and touched the water, fingertips gliding across the surface.

She asked, "Can I ask you a question?"

"Go for it."

"Where are the other counselors?"

Regina felt her throat tighten. She unintentionally held her breath. Kimberly took her hand out of the water and shook it to dry it off. Drops of water hit their legs.

The girl said, "Carol used to talk to me every night before I went to bed. Chase always teased us, but he was a lot of fun. Some of the other counselors aren't around, either, are they? It feels lonelier here. What's happening?"

Regina opened her mouth to speak, but nothing came out. She looked at the sparkling water and thought about diving into the lake for a swim—a swim to shore, a swim away from her problems.

She swallowed the lump in her throat, then she said, "You're a very perceptive girl, aren't you? You don't have to worry about Carol or any of the other counselors. We're taking care of everything."

"Did something bad happen?"

"To be completely honest with you, Kim, I really don't know. But seriously, we're taking care of it. We're going to make sure they're okay and that you're all safe. Mr. Perry has even called for help. The cops will make sure everything is fine. I promise."

"The... cops?" Kimberly repeated, voice stifled by concern and fear. "Doesn't that mean something *really* bad happened? What if everything isn't fine? What happens if they got hurt?"

Regina broke eye contact. To her dismay, she found herself surrounded by happy campers and oblivious counselors. She didn't want to be the camp's killjoy. *Just keep your mouth shut until we close the camp,* she told herself. *Just a few more days.*

She said, "Kim, there's really nothing else we can do right now. No matter what happens, *you* are going to be okay and *I* am going to be by your side. Even if camp ended early—and I'm not saying it is—I'm going to be there for you. I'm still going to give you my phone number and we... we're... I'm just going to be there for you through thick and thin, I promise."

Kimberly frowned and nodded. She could tell Regina was lying. She trusted the counselor, though.

She said, "I understand. Maybe we can call each other before school starts again."

"Sure," Regina replied. "I'd really like that."

"Look," Kimberly said.

Regina glanced over her shoulder. She spotted another rowboat meandering towards them from the opposite end of the lake. Jennifer Rhodes and two campers in matching red swimsuits, Monica and Caitlin, sat in the rowboat. They stopped about fifteen meters away from Regina and Kimberly.

"How's it going, ladies?" Jennifer asked.

"Just enjoying the weather," Regina responded. "How about you three? Getting a good workout?"

Monica flexed her bicep and said, "Always."

The girls laughed. Regina glanced at Kimberly. She looked happy, but she had sucked her lips into her mouth, as if she were afraid of making a sound.

Regina asked, "Hey, Kim, you wanna have a picnic later?"

"A–A picnic?" Kimberly stuttered.

"Yeah. We can eat lunch at the quad or maybe even near the shore. No one's using those benches right now. We can also invite Jennifer, Monica, and Caitlin. Maybe Oscar, too. Three campers, three counselors. I think a small group like that will help you hone your social skills. What do you say, sweetie? You wanna have a picnic?"

Kimberly looked down at herself. She didn't really have to think about the offer. The answer was obvious: '*Yes!*' She didn't want to appear too eager, though. Throughout her short life, she found excitement often led to disappointment.

Fighting the urge to scream, she said, "Sure."

"That's what I like to hear," Regina responded. She glanced over at the other rowboat and shouted, "Hey, ladies! You up for a picnic at lunch?"

Caitlin grinned and, with unbridled enthusiasm, she shouted, "I love picnics!"

"Me too," Monica said.

Jennifer said, "It sounds like we're all on board. We'll see you–"

Jennifer and the girls gasped as the rowboat rocked violently. It looked like they were hit by a strong wave, but the lake was calm. Jennifer stood up and checked the surrounding water while the campers scanned the floor.

Monica asked, "What happened?"

"I think we hit something," Caitlin responded.

"Maybe we hit one of the boys."

"Shush," Jennifer said. "Don't talk like that. It's not funny."

Monica said, "I didn't say you *killed* 'em. Maybe we just bumped into 'em."

Regina and Kimberly watched their rowboat from afar. They noticed the rowboat's shaking and they could see the deep concern on Jennifer's face.

Regina asked, "You ladies okay?"

Eyes on the water, Jennifer said, "Regina, um... Can you see anything under our boat?"

"Like what?"

'*A kid.*' Jennifer didn't want to say it, but she was afraid her rowboat had struck one of the campers. The kids weren't allowed to swim that far out, though.

"Anything," she said.

Regina and Kimberly gazed at the water under Jennifer's rowboat. They didn't see anything under them. Then Regina's pupils dilated with fear.

She said, "I think there's some–"

Jennifer's rowboat flipped. Jennifer, Monica, and Caitlin were flung off it. Caitlin knew how to swim and she wore a life jacket like everyone else, but she came out of the water gasping and whining. She couldn't help but panic.

As she swam to the capsized rowboat, she yelled, "Help! Ha–Help! Please!"

Regina's eyes darted left and right as she searched for Jennifer and Monica. She heard the counselors and campers screaming from the docks and shore, stunned by the sudden accident.

'*Regina! Regina! Regina!*'

She heard the other counselors and campers calling on her to act, but it was as if all of her training and experience had been wiped from her mind. She didn't know what to do because she didn't understand what had just happened.

"Regina!" Kimberly cried as she tugged on the counselor's arm.

Regina snapped out of her contemplation. She looked at Kimberly, then at the capsized rowboat. Caitlin called out to her, too, sobbing hysterically.

Regina removed her life jacket and said, "Stay on the boat, Kim. Please, whatever you do, *stay on the boat*."

She took one step back, then she dove into the lake. She swam over to Caitlin. Her heartbeat was so fast and so strong that she felt like it was responsible for the splashing, rippling water around them.

Caitlin yelled, "She's under the boat!"

Regina said, "Ca–Caitlin, I–I need you to–"

"Monica's under the boat! She's under the boat!"

"Caitlin!" Regina interrupted. There was more fear than frustration in her voice. Caitlin stopped screaming, but she kept whimpering. Regina said, "I'll get her. Swim to Kimberly. Now."

"I'm scared," Caitlin whined.

"It's going to be okay. Kimberly is right there. She's watching you. She'll take care of you. Okay? You understand?"

Caitlin nodded reluctantly, tears and mucus cascading across her face. She took a deep breath, looked left and right as if she were about to cross a busy street, then she swam towards Kimberly. Regina watched her for no more than five seconds, then she drew a deep breath of her own before diving into the water. She saw Monica kicking her legs under the rowboat. The girl screamed as Regina emerged from the water next to her.

The counselor said, "Monica, stop. Please stop. It's me. Monica, it's me!"

Monica kept panicking. Regina shook her shoulders to try to break her fear-induced trance. It didn't work. So, she hugged the girl.

She whispered, "It's okay. I'm here. It's okay." Monica's screaming weakened to some unintelligible whispers. In a soft, understanding voice, Regina said, "We're going to swim back to my rowboat now. Everything's going to be okay. I'll be right next to you the entire time. Can you do this?"

"I–I–I'm sca–scared," Monica stammered.

"I know, I know," Regina responded. "But I *need* you to do this. The sooner you're out of the water, the sooner we can get you back to shore with the others. Can you do this for me, Monica?"

Monica hesitated. She didn't feel safe under the capsized boat with her head out of the water, so she was absolutely terrified of swimming underwater in their current situation. But she trusted Regina.

She said, "Don't let me go."

Regina grabbed the girl's life jacket and said, "I'll be right next to you, sweetie. You ready?"

Monica drew a couple of shaky breaths, then she nodded. Regina returned the nod. They inhaled deeply at the same time, then they plunged into the water. They went under the rowboat.

Regina stopped before they could start swimming up to the surface. She felt like the world was moving in slow motion around them. Underwater bubbles floated around the girls, bobbling towards the surface. The shouting above them—from the other rowboat, from the docks, from the shore—was muffled and sluggish.

Fear had a way of manipulating a person's perception.

Regina spotted Jennifer a few meters below them. Crimson clouds of blood enveloped her body. Like oil from a blowout, blood gushed out of a cavernous gash on her throat. It looked like she was halfway to being beheaded. Despite the plumes of blood swirling around her head, Regina could see her friend's vacant eyes—*her dead eyes*.

There was a large, burly figure behind her. He appeared to be wearing hooded coveralls and a scuba mask. His bright blue eyes shone through his goggles.

A terrifying thought entered Regina's mind: *There's a killer at Camp Blaze.*

Monica pulled on Regina's hair, causing the counselor to wince. Regina looked up at the girl, then down at Jennifer. The killer grabbed a fistful of Jennifer's hair and yanked her head back. The grisly wound on her throat widened. Her cracked spine was exposed. Her head was barely attached to her body by some cracked bones and flimsy piece of flesh at the nape of her neck.

Regina felt her stomach knot up as Jennifer's blood billowed towards her. She knew she couldn't rescue her, but she could still protect Monica and the other campers. She tightened her grip on Monica's life jacket and swam faster. Coughing and groaning, they emerged from the water between the upright rowboat and the capsized one.

Kimberly weaved and bobbed her head for a better view of the water. She furrowed her brow upon noticing Jennifer's absence. Caitlin sat next to her— arms crossed, head shaking, shoulders shivering. Oscar and Kenneth paddled their way to them on separate rowboats.

As she caught her breath, Regina shouted, "Hurry! There's... There's someone in the water! He has Jennifer! Oh my God, hurry! *Help her!*"

A TOWEL DRAPED OVER HER SHOULDERS, REGINA SAT AT the end of a dock and stared absently at the lake. The shimmering water was blinding. A cool breeze carried the lake's crisp scent through the forest. She wasn't captivated by nature's beauty, though. She focused on the ongoing search for Jennifer and the suspected murderer.

Equipped with scuba diving gear, police searched the water for the body of a dead teenager. Some of the senior counselors stayed on the shore to assist the police. Most of the counselors stayed with the campers at their cabins, though. Although most of the campers were unaware of the incident, the counselors were asked to prepare for a potential emergency evacuation.

Regina turned her attention to the other side of the lake. There was a dock on that side, too, but there weren't many cabins over there. From her position, she could only see a toolshed on the opposite shore and a sea of trees. Her eyes moved up. She wondered if Jennifer's killer was watching her from the branches. Then her gaze wandered back to the lake.

Or maybe he's still in the water, she thought as she pulled her feet up.

Tears spilled across her cheeks as she blinked. Images of Jennifer's death—of the gruesome wound on her neck—flashed in her mind. She ran her fingers across her scalp, then she started tugging on her hair while whimpering.

"I'm sorry, Jenny," she whispered. "I'm so sorry."

She heard the dock creaking behind her. She glanced over her shoulder and found Officer Marino and Alvin walking towards her. Marino kept a stern, professional expression on his face. His eyes were dim with disappointment, though. He wasn't completely cold-blooded. Alvin looked depressed, his head hanging down in shame. His frown was so deep that the corners of his mouth almost touched his jaw.

Marino crouched beside Regina and asked, "How you holding up?"

"I'm... I'm okay."

"Are you sure you don't want to see a paramedic?"

"I–I'm fine. I wasn't, um... I didn't get hurt."

Marino said, "Well, I've spoken to Mr. Perry about the situation. I figured you deserved an update, too. You are, after all, at the center of this investigation at the moment."

"The center?" Regina repeated. "Wha–What do you mean? What's going on? Am I... Am I a suspect or something?"

"No, no, no. It's not like that. But you are a... a key witness. Sure, there were a couple of campers around at the time of the incident, but they're kids. Some of them believe in the boogeyman, others might think the Loch Ness Monster is out here. But you... Well, let's just say you are our most reliable witness."

Regina nodded slowly and stuttered, "O–Okay, I... I think I understand. So, um, what was the update? Did you find Jennifer or... or him?"

Marino sniffled, then he said, "I won't sugarcoat it, Ms. Park: We haven't found a thing. We didn't find Ms. Jennifer Rhodes and we didn't find a 'killer in coveralls.' I've had officers going in and out of the lake for hours, we've combed through the woods several times, but... We've found no evidence of foul play."

"*Murder*," Regina hissed. "It was murder, not 'foul play.' And it's not possible. I've been sitting here for hours, too. Your cops go in for a few minutes, then come out for an hour, then go back in for a few minutes. They need to go down there, all the way to the bottom, and they need to stay there until they find her."

Marino said, "We're using every available resource."

"So, what? Are you just going to leave without

finding her or him? What if that killer—*that monster*—is still down there?"

Alvin said, "Regina, darling, you know that's not likely. Even with scuba diving equipment, he wouldn't have enough oxygen to stay down there all day. And we've been watching this lake for hours. You said it yourself, you haven't taken your eyes off it. He can't be down there."

Regina scowled at him and said, "That's bullshit. This is all... It's *bullshit!*" She glared daggers at Marino and said, "How could you lose him? This is supposed to be *your* job. Why can't you just do your damn job?!"

Marino was unbothered by Regina's attitude. As a veteran of the police force, he understood fear, grief, and survivor's guilt. He would have been suspicious if she *wasn't* angry at herself and the world.

He said, "Ms. Park, I need you to listen to me. I interviewed the other counselors. I spoke to some of the kids who were at the dock and shore when the incident occurred. I spoke to Kimberly and those girls you rescued, Monica and Caitlin. I haven't had the chance to thank you for your heroic actions, by the way, so... thank you for that."

Regina rubbed her eyes and said, "Please get to the point."

"Sure, sure. What I'm saying is: No one saw a person in the water or around the lake. No one saw a person in scuba gear drag Ms. Rhodes away. *You* haven't seen him emerge from this lake, either. No one has seen this mysterious individual and that's... that's..."

"Are you saying I made it all up, officer?"

Marino stood up and said, "I'm saying that it's something to think about. We know something happened to Ms. Rhodes or she would have shown up by now, but... Listen, all I'm saying is we will continue our search for her and this mysterious individual. You have my word on that. In the meantime, I'd like you to stay out of the water. Go to a safe place and... collect yourself. Sometimes, during times of tragedy, we miss out on the 'little things.' I want to give you time to heal, and I hope that will help you find those 'little things.' Everything helps in our investigations. Remember that."

Alvin leaned forward and said, "I'm sorry to interrupt with more bad news, Regina, but I think you should know that I've also been advised to shut down the camp as soon as possible. I know how much love you have for the campers and how much work you've put into this place. I wish I could stay open all year, but I'm out of options. I can't have all of this on my conscience. I'm sure you feel the same way. I'm sorry for... for everything."

At heart, Regina was glad the camp was closing ahead of schedule. Guilt and paranoia weighed heavy on her mind. She would miss her friends and the campers, but she was eager to leave. She didn't know how to respond, though. '*Great, when are the buses leaving?'* It sounded audacious to her. So, she stayed quiet.

Alvin said, "I'll be making calls to the campers' guardians throughout the rest of the day. I want you to take it easy. You've been through enough, darling. I'll handle the legwork. You go hit the showers, take a nap, then go to the counselors' cabin and wait for me there. I want to have a meeting with all of you around dusk. Okay?"

Regina nodded. Alvin patted her shoulder, then he beckoned to the police officer.

Marino said, "I'll be in touch."

The cop followed Alvin across the dock. They discussed the closure of the camp. Regina heard another set of approaching footsteps. She glanced over her shoulder and spotted Oscar walking past the other men.

As he approached, Oscar said, "I thought they'd never leave. Those other cops wouldn't let me come over here until he was finished." He sat beside Regina. He grabbed her hand and asked, "How are you doing, Reggie?"

Regina sighed, then she said, "I feel like shit."

"What can I do to help?"

Regina couldn't take her eyes off the water. She couldn't blink, either. She didn't see anyone, but she felt like she was staring at the killer—and the killer was staring back at her.

She said, "I saw someone in the lake, Oscar. I saw

someone in the water. He was a big guy, a–a... a *scary* guy." Her voice broke, so she paused to recompose herself. She licked her lips, then she said, "And I saw him take Jennifer away. She was already... He already cut her when I went down there. Her throat was... slit. Then he pulled her away. There's a killer out here and the cops can't find him. We–We're not safe. God, please believe me."

Regina buried her face in Oscar's chest and sobbed. Oscar wrapped his arms around her and gazed into the lake. Like the rest of the counselors and campers, he didn't see any suspicious people during the incident. At the same time, he couldn't explain the boat's sudden capsizing or Jennifer's mysterious disappearance, either.

He said, "I believe you. We're going to get to the bottom of this."

10

THE MEETING

REGINA SAT ON A SOFA IN THE LIVING ROOM, A WOOL blanket wrapped around her body and a mug of hot chocolate clasped in her hands. Billiard balls *clacked* behind her, a pot *whistled* on the stove in the kitchen to her left, and flames *crackled* in the fireplace in front of her. She saw the silhouettes of two counselors through the sidelights around the front door and heard a couple of counselors walking through the bedrooms upstairs. Everyone was trying to stay occupied.

Oscar sat beside Regina, his hand on her bare knee. He was quiet, gazing at the fireplace with brooding eyes. He had tried to comfort his girlfriend earlier, but he was now out of words—out of optimism. Regina had unintentionally planted seeds of suspicion and doubt in his mind. Her voice echoed through his head: '*There's a killer out here. There's a killer out here. There's a killer out here.*'

What if she's right? he thought.

Kenneth leaned over the kitchen bar and said, "Alvin's late. Maybe we should start this lil' meeting without him, huh?"

Oscar squinted at him, as if he didn't recognize his own friend. He had heard Kenneth's voice, but his words sounded like they were in a different language.

"What'd you say?" he asked.

"*I said* we should think about starting the meeting without Alvin. The guy's late if you haven't noticed."

"For what? *He* called the meeting to talk to *us*. Without him, there is no meeting. Just relax, dude. He'll be here."

"The sun's already going down. As far as we know, the old man probably fell asleep in his office or completely forgot that he told us to meet him here. Besides, there's no harm in talking about what's going on, right? I mean... unless you're scared something is going to be exposed."

"Something?" Oscar repeated. "What the hell's that supposed to mean?"

Kenneth snickered as he walked around the bar. His sneakers thudded on the kitchen's linoleum tiles, then the floorboards groaned under his shoes as he entered the living room. He stopped behind a recliner and leaned over its back-rest. He glanced around the living room and saw everyone staring back at him. He enjoyed the attention.

He said, "Well, my friend, it's kind of obvious, isn't it? Everyone's thinking it, but no one wants to say it."

Flustered, Oscar said, "Then spit it out."

"All right, all right. No need to get hostile, buddy. I'm just saying... Missing counselors, a rowboat 'incident' with one, uh... *suspected* death. If we connect those pieces, we can assume they're all dead, right?"

"They? Who?"

"The missing counselors, doofus. Taylor, Carol, Matt, Chase... No one is saying it, but it's on all of our minds. They were killed and the killer is somewhere around here. Somewhere among us."

"Shut up, Kenny," Oscar responded. "You're just fear mongering. You're trying to cause chaos or, y'know, 'mass hysteria' for your own sick pleasure. And it's not funny. Don't take this too far just for a fuckin' laugh. Now's not the time for that. Go back to the kitchen, get some coffee or hot chocolate, and relax. Alvin will be here soon. I know it."

Kenneth approached the fireplace, shaking his head in disapproval. He was considered the camp clown, he had a knack for telling horror stories and pulling pranks, but he wasn't joking around this time.

As he watched the dancing flames, he said, "You all think I'm playing. You want to believe that I'm joking or building up to some punchline. And it's because you're scared."

Oscar said, "Kenny, I swear you better–"

"It's true," Kenneth interrupted. "You're scared.

We're *all* scared, but none of us want to admit it." He turned his back to the fire. Wagging his index finger at Oscar, he said, "But let me tell you something: *I'm right*. And that killer out there, he could be *in here*. He could be one of us. And you all know it."

Regina looked over her shoulder, then at the kitchen. The other counselors were quiet, captivated by Kenneth's speech. Some of them moved away from each other, looking at one another with distrust, while others appeared saddened by the possibility that their friends had been murdered.

Breaking the silence, Oscar asked, "Like you, Kenneth? Hmm? Could *you* be the killer?"

Kenneth stared at him with a deadpan expression for a few seconds, then he chuckled. Hands in his pockets, he started pacing in front of the fireplace.

He said, "No, it's not me. I'm the... the 'stupid' one, y'know? I'm the douchebag that's supposed to die first. Could be you, Oscar. I mean, you're pretty strong and quick." He nodded at the kitchen and said, "Could be Chelsea over there. She was very close to Chase, wasn't she?"

"Fuck you, asshole," Chelsea snapped as she marched up to the bar.

Kenneth shrugged and laughed. He stopped in front of the coffee table between him and the sofa. He locked eyes with Regina.

He said, "Or maybe it's the person we'd least expect."

"Me?" Regina said wonderingly.

"*You.* You were the last person to see Taylor and Carol, right? And since you're pretty much our manager, you 'let' them leave. But now you claim you don't know where they went. I say that's bullshit. And, again, you're basically our boss. So, *you* put Matt at the back of the line during the obstacle course, didn't you? You–"

"That's enough," Oscar interrupted.

Regina stammered, "It–It–It's not like that."

Kenneth said, "But it is. You put him back there, so you set him up. You were working at the archery range when Chase disappeared, too. Then Jennifer's rowboat 'magically' flipped and some 'big guy' dragged her away underwater. And *you* were the only one to witness all of it. You really expect us to believe all of that?"

Regina's rosy face scrunched up. Her head began to vibrate, as if her skull were about to burst open. Kenneth took a step back, expecting her to unleash an earsplitting screech. Instead, she exhaled shakily through her nose.

"You're dumber than you look," she said. "I let Taylor and Carol go because that's what *they* wanted. I was with you and Oscar at the campfire the *whole* time they were gone. I didn't even know Matt disappeared until the rest of you reported it to Alvin. And I was in front of *you* and Oscar the entire time at the obstacle course. Everyone knows that. As for Chase, you're right about one thing: Chelsea was close to him. She was probably the last person to see him, but I *highly* doubt she did anything to hurt him. And Jennifer... I know what I saw. You might not have seen that man in the water, but *everyone* saw that boat flip on its own. For crying out loud, I don't have telekinetic powers, asshole."

She leaned back in her seat, laughing and crying at the same time. The stress, fear, and grief were too much to handle. She put her hand over her brow and lowered her head to hide her eyes.

She said, "This is bullshit. You want to blame me for doing my job? For being the head counselor? That's so stupid." She glared at him and said, "What about you? Huh? Maybe it was you. Maybe you were jealous of Taylor and Carol. Maybe Chase saw you hurt them and—and you had to tie up loose ends. Maybe you... you cut Jenny and pulled her away because she rejected you. It's easy to make bullshit assumptions, isn't it, you selfish asshole?"

Kenneth said, "Oh, fuck off, Regina. You're not going to twist this with your crocodile tears."

"She saw through you, didn't she? You killed Jenny because she wouldn't—"

"Shut up, bitch! It was you! I know it was you! You're not going to pin this on me. I'm not going to let you make me an outcast so you can... so you... so you can get me alone to try to kill me! You're not laying a finger on me, bitch! If you even *try*, I'll take you out back and–"

"And *what*?" Regina interrupted. "Kill me?"

"You try to touch me and I'll–"

"Stop it!" Oscar said as he jumped to his feet.

Only the sound of the *crackling* fire moved through the old cabin. The counselors were in awe. They had never seen an argument like that at Camp Blaze.

"Is this what you kids do while I'm out?" Alvin asked from the kitchen.

The counselors shared a sigh of relief upon hearing his voice.

───────

Alvin placed a plastic bag full of groceries and a case of beer on the kitchen bar. He didn't have enough time to plan a big party, but he wanted to help his counselors let loose. He walked around the bar, then pointed at the beer and said, "That'll be our little secret. Keep it to *one* beer per person and do *not* let any of the campers see or smell any of it."

Some of the counselors smiled and chuckled. Two guys even shared a high five near the billiards table. They weren't expecting Alvin to show up with alcohol, especially since most of the counselors were under twenty-one years old. Their joy was brief, though. The tension between them lingered. Alvin felt it, too.

The owner said, "I don't know what's going on in

here. You're arguing, that's obvious, but I can't pretend like I caught it all. And I know it doesn't seem right for me to waltz in here with beer like we're celebrating death. I just want you kids to have a good night. One more good night. Some of you are lovers, but all of you are friends, right? You shouldn't be attacking each other like this. Don't waste your time arguing. Don't waste these final hours turning against each other and breaking lifelong friendships."

The counselors stayed quiet, but they all agreed with him. Most of them had attended the camp as campers before returning as counselors. The romance between Regina and Oscar sparked at Camp Blaze three years earlier when they were junior counselors. They had no real reason to suspect or hate each other.

Fear made people irrational.

Kenneth said, "I get what you're saying, Mr. Perry, but it doesn't always work that way. Friends kill friends. We've seen it happen before. There's just too much... *weird* crap going on around here. Someone has to be responsible. If it's not one of us, then we're all sitting in here waiting to be the next victim. Or maybe it'll be one of the campers. They're like sitting ducks in their cabins."

Alvin said, "Calm down, son. We don't need a witch hunt right now. We need solidarity. The cops have been in and out of this place all day. They haven't found a single piece of evidence of murder on our beloved camp. And they'll be back first thing in the morning when the buses arrive for the children. They wouldn't have left all of you here if they thought one of you killed someone." He raised his hands, as if ordered to do so by the police. He said, "So, let me be clear: There is no murderer on campgrounds. I'm positive about that."

A little smile lifted the corners of his mouth as he examined the counselors. Their fear didn't bring him any happiness, but it confirmed his theory.

He said, "You're kids. You are... baby-faced kids. You're part of a softer generation. No offense to the young men in the room, but it's true. I can say with confidence that none of you are capable of killing anyone, let alone butchering your friends."

"You're wrong about that," Kenneth whispered, sneering at the floor.

Regina heard him, but the other counselors missed it. *Sit on it,* she thought. *I can use it against him if he tries to blame me again.*

Alvin said, "Listen, we have a few of the junior counselors sitting in front of the campers' cabins. They have, uh... walkie-talkies and they're keeping a lookout in shifts. If they see something, they'll let you know. And although most of the police won't be back until tomorrow morning, Officer Marino will return to conduct some interviews. And they're only interviews, okay? He won't be here to interrogate anyone. We have everything under control."

"I think we should leave," Kenneth said. "I'd love to

party with everyone, but it doesn't feel right. Why don't we just call some taxis and get out of here?"

Alvin said, "We have buses but no drivers to get the campers out, Mr. Wolf, and those campers are under our supervision until they leave."

"The junior counselors are already watching them. You don't need all of us here."

Oscar said, "If you really think someone's out there, we're going to be a lot safer if we stick together. The junior counselors and campers are watching each other's backs. We can't start splitting up."

"Are you afraid of talking to the police, Kenny?" Regina asked. "Getting nervous?"

Kenneth huffed, then he said, "I'm not afraid of talking to anyone. I *am* afraid of 'disappearing' out here for no reason. I don't want to get caught in a bloody massacre, all right? Hell, if there's a killer out there, what's stopping him from locking us up in here and setting this cabin on fire?"

The other counselors chatted amongst themselves, discussing their options. Regina's gaze went to the door, then to the fireplace. *We are cornering ourselves, aren't we?* she thought.

Alvin said, "All right, all right. Settle down, everyone."

The counselors kept whispering.

'*Should we leave?*'

'*What if there is a killer out there?*'

'*Anyone have any money for a taxi?*'

Alvin said, "I promise you: You're safe. Nothing is going to happen. Grab a drink and a bite to eat. Play some music, play some pool or blackjack, grab my portable DVD player and watch a movie. Wait for Marino and everything will be fine. Just trust me and enjoy yourselves. That's all I ask of you. This night might be your last night at camp anyway."

The counselors were still frightened, but they trusted Alvin. They also felt safe knowing Marino was on his way to Camp Blaze. There wasn't enough beer for them to get inebriated, but they figured it was enough to calm their nerves. They started grabbing drinks and snacks.

Alvin smiled and said, "Thank you." He beckoned to Regina and said, "Take a walk with me, darling."

"Where to?" Regina asked.

"Like I said, Marino and his partner will be here soon. I want to meet them up front. I'm sure Marino has a few more questions for you, too."

"Okay, fine," Regina said. She kissed Oscar's cheek, then said, "I'll be back in a little while. Be careful, okay?"

"I'll be here," Oscar responded.

Regina gave a half-hearted smile and waved at the other counselors, then she followed Alvin out of the cabin.

HOLDING THE BLANKET SNUGLY AROUND HER BODY, Regina walked next to Alvin on the dirt path. The Bears' cabins were to their right. A junior counselor sat in front of each cabin. One of them listened to music on a Sony Walkman while the other tinkered with her walkie-talkie. The lights were still on in the cabins, so everyone could see the campers' silhouettes as they chatted, danced, and roughhoused. The kids knew something was wrong, but they weren't aware of the severity of the situation.

It was just another night at camp for most of them.

Regina heard Alvin's voice, but she paid him no mind. He was rambling on and on about the good ol' days.

A pair of boys, Kyle and Joey, bolted out of the restroom to their right. They were giggling about something.

"*Hey,*" Alvin hissed. The boys instantly stopped laughing. Alvin asked, "What do you think you're doing out here? Didn't you hear? There's a darn curfew."

Kyle stuttered, "Ye–Yeah, we were just–"

"What cabin do you belong to?"

"Um... Bears."

Scratching the back of his head, Joey said, "We were just going to pee and get some air. And the cabin's boring right now. Some of the other kids are already sleeping."

Alvin said, "Well, maybe that's a good idea. Get back to your cabin and get ready for bed. You really shouldn't be out here right now."

Eyes large and curious, Kyle asked, "Why is there a curfew anyway? Is something wrong?"

"It's 'cause of the rowboat accident," Joey said with confidence.

"No, it's not. Why would there be a curfew for an accident, idiot?"

"Don't call me an idiot, *idiot*."

"Then stop being an idiot, you–"

"Stop it," Alvin said, lips trembling with a desire to smile. "It's just getting late and it's almost time for bed. Besides, you wouldn't want the boogeyman to catch you out here, would ya?"

The boys responded with a synchronized one-syllable laugh: '*Ha!*' They didn't believe in the boogeyman. They were just humoring the old man.

Alvin said, "Go on. Get out of here."

He walked forward as the kids scampered away. Regina watched the campers until they reached the Bears' cabins. Even in the face of danger, she put the children's safety over her own. The junior counselor with the Walkman shrugged and waved at Regina, as if to say: '*Sorry about that.*' Then he led the boys into the cabin.

Regina followed her boss' lead. Alvin walked with his hands clasped behind his back. He looked up and smiled at the night sky. He could see a couple of twinkling stars.

"How are you feeling, darling?" he asked. "I hate to say it, but you don't look so good. I see the sadness—the pain—in your eyes. Are you okay?"

"I'm fine," Regina said softly, as if she were afraid her voice would break if she spoke any louder.

"I've known you since you were a kid, since you were as tall as my knee. I can read you like a book, Regina. You've always come to me when you had a problem, and I know you have a problem now. What is it? What's on your mind?"

"It's not *a* problem, Mr. Perry," Regina responded. "I have a *hundred* problems. I mean, seriously, this is... this is all just one big mess and I can't get it off my mind. I don't know if my friends are okay or if they're... if they're all dead. I have no idea if we're in danger right now or if someone is getting killed as we speak. And Kenneth is trying to blame all of this on me. He's probably lying to the other counselors right now, trying to turn everyone against me. It's all just so crazy. It's all a bunch of crap, really. I hate it."

"You have to be more positive, kiddo. I know what you saw in the lake, but there's still hope. Until all of them are found, until we find *undeniable* evidence, we can't allow our fears to create grief and we can't allow that grief to control us. We have to be optimistic. We have to keep our faith alive."

Alvin gave her a hopeful smile. He was worried about the missing counselors, but he didn't let fear hijack his mind.

As he examined the camp, he said, "Oh, how I long for the good ol' days, darling. I know you remember them, too. The kids could go out on their own, exploring the woods and swimming at the lake and... and discovering themselves. And I know many of my counselors 'discovered' themselves, too." He chuckled, trying to lighten the mood. He sighed, then he said, "But the good ol' days are long gone. Have been for a while now, haven't they? These are the... the 'bad new days.' The kids can't go out on their own, can't camp out in the woods, can't swim in the lake, can't discover themselves. And I'm sorry about that, Regina. I wish we could go back to the times when masked killers weren't running around camps and killing innocent people. Lunatics have pushed us into a corner. It's not safe to keep your doors open at night anymore, not safe to travel the woods alone anymore... The world's just not safe these days, is it?"

Regina said, "I don't know about yesterday or tomorrow. I only know about today. And today... today was ugly. And I know we've had a lot of good years here, but from the stories I've heard about the tragedies at Camp Blaze and other camps across the state, I don't think the good ol' days were *that* good anyway. It's just the nostalgia talking. Rose-tinted glasses, y'know?"

"I suppose you're right. There isn't a place in this world that hasn't been touched by tragedy. But Camp Blaze has been a safe place for the past decade. You've seen it yourself. Still, I can't disagree with you. I want to defend this place, my home, but I can't. Nowadays, it's just not safe to walk out here alone at night, especially for a young woman like yourself. You could be hurt by anyone or anything. You're very lucky to have me by your side, Regina. Very lucky, indeed."

An expression of dismay dawned on Regina's face. She lagged behind Alvin as they walked beside the cafeteria. He didn't threaten her, but his words got under her skin. He looked and sounded like he was about to do something he was going to regret.

Regina thought: *Is he responsible for the disappearances? Is he the killer? Is he going to hurt me?*

She found herself trying to link Alvin to the disappearances. She didn't think it was possible for an elderly man to flip a rowboat and kill someone underwater, but she entertained the idea. If she learned anything from life, it was that *anyone* and *everyone* was capable of committing acts of evil.

Noticing Regina was falling behind, Alvin stopped beyond the edge of the cafeteria and turned around to face her, his back to the dark quad. Regina drew back, alarmed. She was hit with a sudden bout of disorientation. She leaned against the cafeteria's entrance to stop herself from collapsing.

Alvin said, "Jesus Christ, Regina, you're pale. Are you okay?"

As the owner took a step towards her, Regina stepped back and said, "Wait. Don't... Please don't move."

"What's wrong, darling?"

Tears stung Regina's eyes. She rubbed her nose and wiped her cheeks as she took three more quicks steps away from Alvin. An epiphany hit her: She couldn't trust anyone. She believed everyone was a suspect, including the people she cared about the most. She finally understood Kenneth's paranoid behavior.

She stammered, "I–I–I have to go back. I have to–"

From around the corner, a man swung a machete down at the owner. The blade severed Alvin's nose and upper lip with one clean chop. The bloody pieces thudded on the ground between Alvin's boots and big drops of blood followed. The old man's lower lip was partially severed, swinging back and forth over his chin like a windshield wiper.

Eyes squeezed shut, Alvin's bloody face crumpled in pain. Blood squirted out of his wounds, sprinkling onto the counselor's face and shirt. He clenched his fists and curled his toes, but he didn't move. He was dazed by the attack.

Regina staggered back and shrieked. Her eyes bulged as a tall, burly man in a white mask emerged from around the corner. He stepped behind Alvin and towered over him. She recognized his hooded coveralls and vibrant blue eyes, but he was bigger than she remembered. *The killer from the lake,* she thought.

Snorting and grunting, Alvin turned to face the masked man. He looked up at his attacker's wide, zany eyes and, for the first time in his life, he felt like he was meeting the embodiment of true evil. The blood cascading over his dentures sprayed out as he tried to speak, but he couldn't pry his own mouth open. His teeth just kept grinding against each other.

The killer gripped Alvin's neck and pushed him towards Regina. Regina screamed as she teetered back. Her legs tangled and she fell on her ass, the blanket landing behind her.

"No! Don't!" she cried.

To her utter surprise, instead of attacking her, the killer pushed Alvin into the cafeteria. For a split second, she thought about running in there to help him. But she knew the cafeteria was empty. She couldn't overpower the masked man on her own. He was a giant compared to her. She had to get help and warn the others.

As she scrambled to her feet, she shouted, "Help!" She lurched away from the cafeteria and began retracing her steps. Slipping and sliding, she yelled, "Oh my God, help! Somebody help! He's here! He's killing him! *Help!*"

The killer dragged Alvin into the narrow kitchen. Alvin's tongue stuck out of his mouth as he gasped for air. The killer pushed the owner down to his knees. He glanced around and examined his surroundings. He peeked into a stockpot on a stove to his left. It was full of beef stew. He turned on the stove, then opened a drawer to his right. He rifled through it, silverware clinking and clanking inside.

Before the killer could grab anything, Alvin tried to stand up. The masked man pushed him back down to his knees. Gasping and groaning, Alvin struggled to his feet once again.

The killer grabbed the nape of Alvin's neck and pushed him down to his hands and knees. He swung his machete at Alvin's right ankle. His heel cord was severed with a wet *crunching* sound. The Achilles tendon slithered up his leg, then back down, and then up again, like a bungee cord. Alvin let out a raspy gasp, then hit the floor face-first.

The masked man chopped Alvin's other ankle with the machete. The old man's legs were so thin—so frail —that his foot was nearly lopped off with one chop.

Stabs of pain shot up his legs. He wanted to scream, but he could only groan and gasp. His feet splashed in a puddle of blood as his legs shook violently.

With Alvin immobilized, the killer reached into the drawer and groped about for a useful tool. *Spoons? Forks? Knives?* The silverware didn't interest him. He opened the neighboring drawer and pulled a box grater out. He took a knee on Alvin's back. He grabbed the back of the old man's head, fingers sinking into his loose forehead and scalp, and lifted it up from the floor.

"N–N–No," Alvin rasped weakly.

The killer pressed the box grater—the side with the largest holes—against Alvin's face. Folds of flabby skin entered the holes. The killer started grating his face, pushing and pulling on the tool. The skin tore off his forehead and cheek. The edge of his eyebrow was detached. Bloody strips of skin, like string cheese dipped in runny mozzarella sauce, hung from his face. Some pieces of flesh spiraled to the floor, piling up like autumn leaves.

Pain shot through Alvin's head, like a bullet zigzagging through his brain endlessly. A tingly sensation spread across his face and scalp. He tried to jerk his head away, but bits of his skin were tangled in the grater's holes. The killer was happy to give him a hand. He tugged on the box grater until it detached from Alvin's face. Flaps of skin hung from the holes.

He turned the box grater, then pressed the side

with the smaller holes against Alvin's left cheek. He started shredding his face again. The skin made a *crinkling* sound as it tore. Fine strips of flesh fell to the floor. Due to his resistance, the box grater slid across Alvin's face. It ate away at the remaining stub of cartilage he called his 'nose' and tore off his lower lip. The grater made a screeching sound as it ground against his dentures. It sliced up his upper gums, too.

The killer dropped the box grater, leaned forward, and inspected Alvin's face. The old man had blacked out during the attack. Some skin remained on his forehead and chin, but most of his face was gone.

The killer leaned in close to Alvin's ear and whispered, "Just like Ash."

He pulled Alvin up to his feet and dragged his limp body to the stove. He threw the lid off the stockpot, then dunked Alvin's face into the boiling beef stew. The stew bubbled. Alvin's blood turned it into a violet liquid. But he didn't put up much of a fight. The old man barely twitched.

The killer held him down for three uninterrupted minutes. Alvin collapsed as soon as his head was pulled out of the stockpot. His mushy face was covered in blood and stew. He kept twitching, but he wasn't breathing.

The masked man casually walked out of the cafeteria, as if he had just finished eating dinner. Although she was long gone, he followed Regina's trail.

12

EVACUATE

REGINA SLIPPED IN FRONT OF THE BEARS' CABINS, landing on her side in the mud. Out of breath, she rolled onto her hands and knees and looked behind her. She was surprised to see the killer wasn't directly behind her. She got to her feet, lost her footing and dropped to her knees, then got up again and lurched towards the closest cabin.

"Run!" she yelled. "You have to run!"

Isaac Cervantes, a seventeen-year-old junior counselor, sat on the porch steps to the boys' cabin and listened to music on his Walkman. He bobbed his head to *The Way I Am* by Eminem while mouthing the lyrics. He didn't notice Regina until she showed up in the periphery of his vision. He glanced at her and immediately flinched. The sweat, tears, mud, and blood all over her worried him.

He got up, lowered his headphones to the nape of

his neck, and stepped back until his back was against the cabin's front door. The chorus to the song blared from his headphones. Regina slowed down as she approached the porch, each step getting heavier and heavier. As she caught her breath, Isaac fiddled with his CD player. He skipped a song, then another, and then finally paused the music.

"Wha–What the hell happened?" he stuttered. "A–Are you... Is that blood? Holy shit, are you bleeding?"

Regina bent over and wheezed in front of him for a couple of seconds. The short sprint and the debilitating fear took her breath away. She looked back at the path again. The masked killer was nowhere in sight. She shambled up the porch steps.

Jabbing her finger at Isaac's chest, she said, "You have... to get out of here. Gather all of the kids in your... in your cabins and get to the buses." She pointed to her left and said, "Take the long way. You hear me? Wa–Walk through the woods if you have to, but whatever you do, *don't* go near the cafeteria. You understand me?"

"What the hell's going on, Regina?"

"Just listen to me! Get everyone from the Bears' cabins to the buses. That's all you need to know right now. I'll explain everything later. Get into the buses, don't turn on any lights, and stay very quiet. Okay? *Okay?*"

"O–Okay," Isaac stuttered as he nodded. "Just... Can't you tell me what's going on? I mean, we're not supposed to go anywhere near the buses without you or one of the other senior counselors or Mr. Perry. Did... Wait a second, did Mr. Perry tell us to evacuate? Was there some sort of accident? Is it a fire? Is the camp burn–"

"*Just listen,*" Regina hissed. "There is a dangerous man walking around here. Avoid anyone you don't recognize. Stay together and get to the buses." As she ran off, she shouted, "Evacuate, Isaac! Take the long way! And don't trust anyone!"

Isaac jogged down the porch steps, but he didn't follow Regina. He dug his fingers into his hair and watched her, baffled by their conversation. He looked over at the junior counselor, Janet Andrews, sitting in front of the other cabin. Janet had heard most of Regina's screaming. '*Evacuate!*' That word sent a chill down her spine. Evacuations were usually linked to grave danger. The counselors shrugged at each other, then they raced to get the campers to the buses.

Regina swiped at her nose as she approached the Gators' cabins. Keila Rodriguez, a red-haired junior counselor, sat in front of the first cabin. She gasped upon spotting Regina. The head counselor looked like a dead woman who had just risen from her grave.

"Keila," Regina said as she stopped at the bottom of the porch. "Keila, I... Get the kids and take them to the buses. Don't... Don't go near the cafeteria, okay? Isaac and the–the Bears... They're waiting for you. Isaac will explain everything."

Brow raised in confusion, Keila asked, "Is something wrong?"

"We're evacuating the camp, okay?"

"Okay, um... Yeah, okay. Let me call Mr. Perry first. He told us to wait here and keep a lookout. We're not supposed to–"

Regina grabbed Keila's shoulders and said, "He's gone. He's... He's gone."

"Wha–What?"

Voice shaking, Regina said, "He was attacked. I think... I think he's dead." Keila inhaled sharply and raised her hands over her mouth. Regina said, "There's a dangerous person at camp. He's wearing a white mask. Stay away from him. Get all of the campers to the buses and wait for me there. Don't turn on the lights and stay very quiet. And if that man goes anywhere near you... drive away."

Keila said, "But we're not supposed to drive the buses. I don't even know how to drive."

"You won't be the only counselor there. I know Isaac has his driver's license or a permit or something like that. He knows enough to get you all out of here. Just go. I have to warn the others."

As the head counselor began to run off, Keila said, "Wait."

Regina let out an exasperated sigh as she slid to a stop. *Stop running your mouth and start running to the damn buses,* she wanted to say.

She glared at her and said, "You *need* to do this. You're responsi–"

"I know, I know," Keila interrupted. "It's just that... I saw Ricky and Maribel sneaking off a few minutes ago. You won't find them at the counselors' cabins."

Goggle-eyed, Regina asked, "Where did they go?"

"Mr. Perry told us not to leave the campers alone, so I couldn't follow them. They were heading to the lake, though. I'm sorry. I should have reported them when I saw them. I screwed up big time."

Regina whispered, "The lake? The lake... *The boathouse.*" She said, "Get everyone out of here, Keila. I'll get Ricky and Maribel, then I'll be right behind you. I promise."

Regina ran off and headed to the shore.

Ricardo 'Ricky' Garcia ran his fingers through his slick black hair, smirking. He took off his brown leather jacket, revealing his plain camp uniform. He threw the jacket over his date's shivering shoulders. Blushing, Maribel Hernandez twirled her curly hair as she walked beside him. She was a petite woman, barely reaching up to Ricky's armpit.

They approached the boathouse just beyond the docks. It looked like a shed hidden under some tall trees.

They stopped in front of the door. Ricky stroked Maribel's chin and kissed her. Without taking his lips off hers, he dug into his pockets, keys and coins *jingling* inside.

He pulled a keyring out and asked, "Ready for some fun?"

Maribel batted her eyelashes at him and said, "Can't wait."

"Run!" a woman's voice echoed across the lake.

"What the hell was that?" Ricky asked.

Maribel looked into the woods, shrugged, and said, "I have no idea."

"Ricky! Maribel!" the woman shouted. "You have to run!"

Maribel sidestepped until her shoulder hit Ricky's chest. She said, "She said our names. That voice said our names."

As he peered into the woods, he said, "I think that's... Is that Regina?"

Regina appeared at the top of a short hill. She lumbered down, shoes sinking into the mud with each step.

Ricky shouted, "We're not going anywhere! It's our turn at the boathouse! You and Oscar can have it tomorrow!"

Regina made it down the hill and wobbled towards them. Maribel got closer to Ricky. Their peer's erratic behavior made her uneasy.

Barely audible, Regina said, "We have... We have to... go. We have to... get to the... buses." She stopped in front of them, put her hands on her knees, and breathed deeply. She said, "You can't stay. We have to leave. He's coming."

Ricky turned his back on her and said, "Let him come. I'm not scared of Alvin." As he put the key in the lock, he muttered, "I'm tired of his bullshit anyway."

"No, he's not... he's..."

Regina's words turned into an incomprehensible babble as Ricky opened the door. She whimpered, then she laughed deliriously. She was tired and terri-fied. She wanted to abandon them—to abandon *everyone*—and flee from the camp on her own. But something inside of her stopped her. Her survival instincts were trumped by her compassion.

My damn heart, she thought.

Upon noticing the blood on Regina's clothing, Maribel tugged on Ricky's arm and whispered, "Hey, look. I think something's seriously wrong."

Ricky ran his eyes over Regina's body. He didn't see any wounds on her, so he figured it was someone else's blood or part of an elaborate prank.

He asked, "What happened to you?"

Regina took two unsteady steps back as she stood straight. She said, "Alvin... I think Alvin is dead. Some maniac in a white mask a–attacked him with a fuckin' machete. He dragged him into the cafeteria and I... I–I couldn't help him. I couldn't do it. I had to run. I–I didn't want to, but *I had to.*"

Ricky and Maribel stared at Regina for a moment,

then they looked at each other. Maribel giggled softly while Ricky's entire body moved with his obnoxious laughter. They didn't believe her. *A camp owner killed with a machete by a maniac in a white mask?* It sounded like something straight out of a horror movie.

As he recomposed himself, Ricky said, "Jeez, Regina, take a bow. I didn't think you had it in you. Who put you up to this? It was Kenneth and Oscar, right? Are they going to show up and 'kill' us, too?" He reached for Regina's shirt, but she staggered away and scowled at him. Ricky said, "Relax. I just wanted to feel the 'blood.' What is it? Ketchup? Paint?"

"This isn't a stupid joke," Regina said, face twitching with rage. "That bastard came out of nowhere and attacked Alvin. I saw Alvin's face... I saw that monster cut Alvin's face off. It's not safe here. Follow me, damn it. Please."

Ricky's smile faded slowly as he gazed into Regina's eyes. He saw the sorrow and agony haunting her gentle soul. *She's telling the truth*, he thought. He wanted to believe she was being pranked, too, but no one at the camp was mean-spirited enough to watch her suffer like that for a laugh—not even Kenneth. He remembered hearing about serial killers slaughtering people at night, teenagers shooting up schools, and the camp's past history of violence.

In a world full of wickedness, a masked man killing people off at a camp didn't seem beyond the realm of possibility.

He said, "If someone is really out here killing people, I think we should just leave on a speedboat. He can catch us on land, but he can't swim faster than a boat, right? What are we waiting for? Let's go."

Regina grabbed his hand and said, "We can't just leave everyone else behind. I haven't warned the other counselors yet."

"We'll take the speedboat up to another cabin as fast as we can, we'll find a radio, and we'll call the others."

"We can't do that. I could have left without warning anyone as soon as I saw that monster, but I didn't and I'm not leaving now. We can't just abandon them."

"Survival of the fittest, Regina. It's that simple. Right, Maribel?"

Maribel glanced at her boyfriend, then at Regina, then back at her boyfriend. She cared about her friends, but her own survival concerned her the most.

She said, "We should go while we have the chance. In horror movies, the person who wants to play the hero... they always die first. I don't wanna die, Regina. I'm no hero and I... I just don't wanna die."

Regina shook her head in disbelief and said, "You're basing your decision on horror movies? You have to be kidding me."

"She's basing her decision on common sense," Ricky said. "You don't run towards danger, you run *away* from it. So, let's start running."

Ricky entered the boathouse. Moonlight entered the room through the doorway, illuminating the speedboat parked in the water. He hurried to the workbench hugging the wall to his right and searched for the boat key.

"I can't see shit in here," he said. "Hit the lights, will ya?"

Maribel looked at Regina with pleading eyes, as if to say: '*Please turn on the lights for us.*' Regina crossed her arms and shook her head. She refused to help them abandon the rest of the counselors and campers. Yet, she stuck around and waited for them, like an overprotective mother refusing to leave her children until she was absolutely certain they were safe.

Maribel sighed in disappointment, then she entered the boathouse. She tapped the wall to her left and searched for the light switch. The floorboards groaned under her feet, the wall thudded with each tap, and the water splashed behind her. Then she heard a clack as she touched a plastic switch plate.

"I think I found it," she said.

"Great," Ricky responded. He turned around and said, "Let there be light."

Maribel flicked the switch. The bulbs on the ceiling flickered for a few seconds, then steadied. Ricky and Maribel gasped at the same time. Regina's mouth hung ajar while her arms dropped to her sides in defeat. The masked killer stood near the speedboat.

"Impossible," Regina said faintly. "You were... at the cafeteria. You can't be here. He–He can't be here."

Jaw trembling, Ricky stuttered, "Wh–Who the hell are you? Wha–What are you..."

His voice faded as he caught a glimpse of the keychain in the killer's hand. The killer raised the keychain up and shook it like a baby rattle, as if to say: '*Looking for this?*'

Ricky said, "Please don't–"

The killer ran forward. He grabbed Ricky's throat and slammed him against the wall next to the door. Maribel shrieked and stumbled into the corner. Her knees buckled, straightened, then buckled again before her legs gave out. Fear crippled her. Regina stepped away from the doorway, eyes wide with fear. She froze up, unable to move or scream.

The killer thrust the long, jagged key into Ricky's right eye. Although it didn't burst, his eyeball made a *popping* sound as the key punctured it. A frightening darkness invaded the right side of his vision while a throbbing headache attacked his right temple. Ricky thrashed about against the wall while turning his head every which way. Only guttural groans came out of his strangled throat.

"No!" Maribel cried. "No! No! No! Stop! Stop it!"

Slimy blood leapt out of his mutilated eye as the killer turned the key to his left. Strings of blood hung over Ricky's cheek. The killer turned the key to the right. A splash of blood flew out of his eye socket and landed on the killer's mask. The inner part of Ricky's eye—the hollowed out vitreous chamber—was left exposed. A gelatinous liquid mixed with blood glistened inside.

The killer pulled the key out, then without any hesitation, he thrust it at Ricky's other eye. The key cut his eye before sliding under it. The sclera reddened, bright like a taillight. The key was wedged between his eyeball and eye socket. The killer pushed the bow of the key down, forcing the tip up *into* Ricky's eye. He looked like he was trying to *scoop* his eye out.

Ricky passed out as the muscles attached to his eye began to tear. His eye slid out over his lower eyelid and sat on his cheekbone. But it remained attached by the optic nerve.

The killer released his grip on Ricky's throat. Legs like noodles, Ricky collapsed. He snored while squirming on the floor.

As the masked man marched towards her, Maribel shouted, "No! Please! Regina, help! He–"

The killer grabbed a fistful of her hair and pulled her away from the corner. He dragged her to the speedboat, then pushed her to the floor. Over the edge of the dock, he thrust her head into the water in front of the boat. She grabbed the edge of the dock and tried to push herself up, but she couldn't overpower him. Her hand slid off and landed in the water, too.

Regina cycled through her options. *Push the killer into the water and save Maribel?* She wasn't sure if she could overpower him. And even if she succeeded, she wasn't sure if it was enough to stop him. He could have easily pulled Maribel into the water with him. *Grab Ricky and help him to safety?* Although only his eyes were damaged during the attack, she knew he couldn't walk on his own and she wasn't strong enough to carry him.

She heard the water bubbling and sloshing as Maribel slowly drowned. Her legs flopped, knees and feet smashing into the floor repeatedly.

Regina refused to be a victim. It pained her to leave, but she convinced herself that she would be able to help more people if she survived.

"I'm sorry," Regina whimpered before running off.

Even as she lurched through the woods, she could hear the splashing water—*the murder*—behind her. She stumbled back onto the path. Bawling her eyes out, she headed back to the counselors' cabin.

13

HE'S COMING

FOLLOW THE LIGHT, Regina told herself.

Tears blurred her vision, but she could still see the light pouring out of the counselors' cabin. She sprinted towards it, exerting every last bit of her energy to push through the finish line. Unable to stop herself, she slammed her body against the front door. The door swung open and she spilled to the floor in the doorway.

She was wheezing, as if someone had just tried to strangle her. She grabbed the doorknob and pulled herself up to her feet.

Oscar sat at the center of the couch between two other counselors. Ridley Scott's *Gladiator* played on the portable DVD player on the coffee table in front of them. Some counselors were playing a game of billiards while the rest of them were socializing in the kitchen. They all stopped their activities because of Regina's dramatic entrance.

They were surprised by her appearance, too. Mud was caked on her knees and dirt was powdered on her thighs. Her uniform was dirty, bloody, and disheveled. Her lips were pale, eyes bloodshot, and hair tousled.

Oscar ran to her side and said, "God, Regina. Sit down." He looked back at the counselors and shouted, "Get me a blanket or a towel! Get me *something!*"

The counselors gathered in the living room, eyes sharp with a combination of caution and suspicion. Kenneth placed his can of beer on a console table, then he slunk towards the kitchen bar. He was getting ready to escape through the back door.

He stuttered, "Wha–What did you do, Regina? Hmm? You're covered... You–You're... Jesus Christ, what the hell did you do, you bitch?!"

"Hey!" Oscar shouted. "Watch your mouth, asshole!"

"She's covered in blood!"

"That doesn't mean jack shit."

"You're a real retard, aren't you? Or–Or–Or you're in this with her, right? That's it. You've been helping her, haven't you?"

Oscar said, "Dude, shut up. This isn't the time for that."

Regina shook her head and sniffled, then she sneered at Kenneth. His insensitive comments disgusted her. In less than one hour, she had witnessed the murder of the camp owner and a brutal attack on two of her peers. Kenneth and the other counselors were comfortable in their luxury cabin while she was out there fighting for survival.

Voice raspy from all of her sobbing, she said, "I didn't hurt anyone, Kenny. I swear to you, to all of you, I didn't hurt a single person. I–I tried to... to save them. You were right. *We* were right. It's just like I said: There's a killer out there."

Oscar cocked his head back and asked, "What did you just say? Did you see him again, Regina? The man from the lake?"

The other counselors erupted in a chorus of whispers, gossiping amongst themselves.

Regina said, "There's a killer out there. He was wearing... He was a big guy dressed like a fuckin' janitor in a white mask. He, um... He killed Alvin. He cut his... face off, then he took him into the cafeteria. It happened right in front of me, I swear. I tried warning everyone else. I told the Bears and the Gators to go to the buses. But Ricky and Maribel, they snuck off. I had to go get them, but that monster was already in the boathouse waiting for them. I didn't see it, I had to run, but I think... I think they're dead. He was so fast, so strong, so... *so evil*. We have to get out of here."

While the other counselors discussed their possible escape routes, Kenneth shouted, "Enough! You're lying to us!"

"I'm not," Regina said.

"You said he took Alvin into the cafeteria. How the hell did he get to the boathouse without catching you first? What? Huh? Did he teleport ahead of you? No, no. There is no man dressed like a janitor out there. No man in a mask. It was you. It's always been you."

"N–No. It wasn't me, I swear."

"*It was you*. It's the only logical explanation."

"Relax," Oscar said in a calm tone. "Everything is under control."

"Under control?!" Kenneth repeated, flustered. "Your girl just said Alvin is *dead*. She said Ricky and Maribel are *dead*. Our friends are dying, Oscar, and she's the only thing linking all of them together. How the hell is everything under control?"

"If you're right—and that's a big '*if*'—then your prime suspect is right here. She can't overpower all of us. I can sit with her right there on that sofa and all of you can keep your eyes on us. As long as we stick together and stay in this cabin, no one will get hurt. Right?"

Kenneth was skeptical while Regina wholeheartedly agreed with Oscar. She closed the door behind her and turned the lock, then she peeked out the sidelight. The killer was nowhere in sight.

She said, "I already started evacuating the cabins. I told the junior counselors to take the kids to the buses and wait for as long as possible. If we have a radio, we can call the Hawks and tell them to go to the buses, too. We tell them to wait until the cops show up or drive off if they see anyone they don't recognize. And the rest of us wait here just like Oscar said. We watch each other's backs."

Oscar nodded and said, "Sounds like a plan. I think there's a–"

"Chelsea, wait!" Kenneth shouted as he ran to the kitchen island.

The counselors turned their attention to the commotion. Chelsea and two friends—Jordan and Andrea—ran out through the kitchen door. Minds infected with distrust, they refused to stick around. They figured they were better off away from Regina and the others.

Kenneth didn't yell at them because he was concerned about their safety. He just couldn't decide if he should stay in the cabin or flee with them.

Regina said, "Close that door. Lock it."

"Shut up," Kenneth hissed as he walked around the kitchen island while pointing at Regina.

All eyes were on him now.

Oscar approached the kitchen bar and said, "Don't do anything stupid, man. You don't know who or what is out there, but you know us. You're safer here. Don't run. Please, man, don't do it."

Kenneth stepped back. He crashed into a counter behind him, startling himself. He looked down at the sink, then at the window above it, then at the door to his left. His breathing intensified and his blinking accelerated. Life-or-death decisions were usually accompanied by an extreme fear of death.

Oscar said, "If you think Regina or I had anything to do with this, your best bet is to stay with us. Keep your eye on us, y'know? And if a killer is out there, he wouldn't dare come in here and try to kill all of us. He's probably some psycho serial killer, but I don't think he's stupid or desperate. Everyone who's died or disappeared, they were alone and isolated. You know it's true, man."

Kenneth sighed and nodded. Oscar's rationale made sense to him. *The police are on the way, too,* he thought. *I just have to survive for a little while longer.*

He said, "Fine, I'll stay. But we have to lock the doors and barricade all the windows. And her." He extended his arm over the kitchen island and pointed at Regina. He said, "We tie her up and we have someone watching her at all times. No, we have two or three people watching her. We can't let her get the upper hand."

Regina said, "No way. I'm not going to let you tie me up with a psychopath on the loose."

"Why not? Didn't you just hear your boyfriend? If the killer is out there, if 'he' even exists, he wouldn't dare come in here. But if you're the killer... then we need to protect ourselves. This cabin is huge. We can't have you walking around here all willy-nilly."

"I'll sit on that recliner and every single one of you can watch me from every angle, but I'm not going to–"

The counselors winced as an arrow broke through the kitchen window. The arrow skewered Kenneth's right shoulder, breaking his bones, butchering his muscles, and bursting the fluid-filled sac at the joint. Blood dripped from the arrowhead while the fletching stuck out from his back. Blood plopped on the kitchen island in front of him and streamed down his back and right arm.

"Wha–What the hell?" Kenneth muttered dazedly while his fellow counselors panicked in the living room.

"Run!" Regina cried. "Kenny, run!"

Another arrow *whooshed* through the broken window. It struck Kenneth's upper back. The second projectile entered his torso between a pair of ribs and punctured his right lung. The arrowhead exited between another set of ribs and stuck out of his chest. During the attack, over their gasping and squealing, the counselors had heard the muscles between Kenneth's ribs tearing. It was a moist *crunching* sound.

Kenneth fell over the kitchen island. He tried to speak, but he was immediately interrupted by a violent coughing fit. Drizzles of blood sprayed out of his mouth with each cough.

"Get down!" Oscar yelled as he crouched behind the bar.

Regina joined him. The other counselors hit the floor, screaming and panting. They crawled under the billiards table and hid behind the sofas.

Oscar peeked out from behind the bar and shouted, "Kenny! Kenneth! Get over here, man! Get away from the windows!"

He retreated behind the bar as another arrow soared through the broken kitchen window. It missed Kenneth, flew over the kitchen bar, and hit the recliner in the living room.

Regina pulled on Oscar's arm and said, "We have to go."

"We can't leave him," Oscar responded.

He peeked around the bar again. He spotted Kenneth leaning over the kitchen island, groaning ghoulishly with a thick string of slimy blood hanging from his bottom lip.

Before he could say a word, the back door burst open. A person in hooded coveralls and a white mask stood in the doorway, holding a claw hammer in his gloved hand. He marched into the kitchen and swung the hammer at the back of Kenneth's head. Blood sprinkled out of a gash on his scalp.

Like a bobblehead doll, the counselor's head swung back and forth. His legs went limp, sneakers sliding across the tiles. His upper body fell on top of the kitchen island, sending plates and silverware plummeting to the floor.

The killer grabbed Kenneth's good shoulder in one hand to pin him down against the kitchen island. He swung the hammer at the back of Kenneth's head four more times. A piece of his scalp flew off his skull and landed on the floor. A spiky lock of hair stuck out of it, hard as a rock thanks to his gel.

Mouth overflowing with saliva and tears racing down her cheeks, Regina yelled, "Stop it! Stop! Don't kill him!"

Some of the counselors sprinted out through the front door while others screamed, frantic with fear. One of the young men grabbed a cue stick. He was too scared to run into the kitchen and attack the intruder by himself, though.

Kenneth fell to his knees. The killer grabbed a fistful of his hair and yanked his head back. Another chunk of the counselor's scalp came off. Then the killer thrust Kenneth's head forward, smashing the counselor's face against the sharp edge of the granite countertop. His nasal septum was crushed. Blood gushed out of a gash on the bridge of his nose, cascading over the thin white strings of sebum coming out of his blackheads.

The killer kept slamming Kenneth's face against the countertop. The counselor's face bounced off it with an unnerving *thud* each time. The cut on his nose widened and spread to his cheeks. His eyes and cheeks swelled up. His skin turned dark red, matching the color of his blood. Then his face started turning blue and purple. And after the sixth slam, the cut on the bridge of his nose looked black. His blood puddled under him and surrounded the kitchen island.

The counselor's nose was mashed into a bloody

nub and his eyes were swollen shut. His mouth hung open, revealing his chipped teeth. His bloody, bumpy, bruised face was unrecognizable.

After the twelfth blow, the masked man released his grip on Kenneth's head. The counselor fell to his side, limp and lifeless. The killer turned around and grabbed a chef's knife from the bamboo knife block next to the sink. He was consumed by a desire to kill—an insatiable bloodlust.

Two more counselors exited the cabin through the front door. A young man ran up the stairs to the bedrooms. The others stayed in the living room, a spell of unshakeable fear keeping them stuck in place. Oscar and Regina walked backwards as the killer strode towards them. Regina kept her eyes on him while Oscar searched for a weapon. His options were limited, so he grabbed the portable DVD player and held it over his shoulder, ready to swing it at him.

As the killer entered the living room, Regina whispered, "No, no, no."

She closed her eyes as she bumped into the sofa. Oscar grabbed her shoulder and yelled at her, but she didn't hear his voice. She didn't hear anything around her. For a moment, she vanished into the darkest recesses of her mind. It was her brain's way of trying to protect her. If death was coming, she didn't want to see it.

Then she flinched upon hearing a deafening gunshot. Two more gunshots quickly followed. A cup shattered in the kitchen. The knife *clacked* as it hit the floorboards in front of her.

Regina's eyes opened to a squint, then widened. She found herself sitting on the sofa's armrest. Oscar was hugging her, using himself as a human shield. She watched as the killer teetered around, one hand on his shot shoulder and the other on his shot thigh. Then the masked person fell to his knees near the kitchen bar.

"Don't move! Don't move!" a man shouted from the front door.

Regina glanced over her shoulder. She saw Marino standing in the doorway with his handgun drawn. A nervous smile and a devastated frown played tug-of-war with her lips. She leaned against Oscar's chest and cried.

14

"10-52, AMBULANCE NEEDED," MARINO SAID, HOLDING A radio up to his mouth. "Suspect has been shot once in the shoulder and once in the leg but is in stable condition."

The masked killer was seated in the sofa in front of him. Quick, raspy breaths emerged from behind his expressionless mask. A coat of cold sweat shimmered on his eyelids. He was handcuffed, his trembling hands clasped over his thighs. Pressure bandages were wrapped around his gunshot wounds to control the bleeding.

Despite the stabs of pain surging from his injuries, the killer gave Marino a death stare. Murder was the only thing on his mind.

Most of the surviving counselors gathered near the billiards table, gossiping about the murderer. Oscar and Regina stood near the front door, arms wrapped around each other. Marino had saved them from the killer, but they couldn't feel the tiniest bit of relief after witnessing Kenneth's violent murder. His body was now covered by a thin blanket.

The same thought ran through all of their minds: *Who is the killer?*

Marino gazed into the suspect's eyes as he wiped his bloody hands with a handkerchief. The killer's glare didn't scare him, though. He looked over his shoulder as two cops entered the cabin through the front door—Ian Miller and Max Bishop.

Marino beckoned to them and said, "There's a body in the kitchen. There are three counselors running around out there and there should be dozens of campers in the buses at the camp's Departure Zone. I haven't had the chance to clear out the second story here, either." He looked at Regina and said, "But I've been told that every counselor has been accounted for."

Bishop drew his handgun and said, "I'll clear out the second floor."

Marino nodded at Miller and said, "I'll take the suspect to a patrol car. You hang back and evacuate this ca–"

"Wait," Regina interrupted, her teary eyes glued to the suspect. "Please just wait a second. We've... Listen, we've been through hell this week. Our friend, Kenny, he's... he's dead in the kitchen. We saw him die. And we saw this *monster* kill him. We deserve answers. I don't want to see this bastard's face on the news next week. I want to see it right *fuckin'* now. Take his mask off."

Oscar said, "She's right. She's always been right. She warned us about him and we ignored her. He killed our friends and our boss. And now that he's caught, you're standing there putting bandages on him and calling an ambulance for him. That's bullshit and you know it."

"It's just protocol," Marino responded.

"Protocol? It's protocol to treat a killer better than his victims? Are you serious, man?"

Marino sighed and shook his head. He felt the unrest in the room. Fear and anger were the key ingredients to every uprising—and there was plenty of fear and anger in that cabin. He looked at the suspect. He sat there like the villain in an episode of *Scooby Doo*, waiting to be unmasked.

Marino asked, "What's your name?" The killer responded with more hoarse breathing. Marino took a step forward and asked, "Did you attack these kids?"

"Oh, c'mon!" a male counselor shouted from behind the billiards table. "You saw him with that knife, dipshit!"

"He killed Kenny!" a young woman yelled.

Regina said, "You know what he did. Stop wasting time. Take off his mask."

"Just do it already," Oscar said.

The counselors assaulted the officers with their

demands while barking insults at the killer. While his partners attempted to control the crowd, Marino examined the quiet suspect. He noticed a lock of dirty blonde hair sticking out from between the hood of the killer's coveralls and his mask. He reached forward slowly, as if he were about to pet an angry dog.

The suspect didn't resist as Marino pushed his hood back and removed his mask. The counselors' clamoring died down as they ran around the sofa for a better view. Their anger waned, replaced by utter astonishment.

The killer was a middle-aged woman.

Her short hair was styled in a bob. Drenched in sweat, a thick lock hung over her forehead. She had crow's feet around her eyes and wrinkles branched out from the corners of her lips. She was pale and sweaty due to her gunshot wounds, but she otherwise looked healthy.

"I know you, don't I?" Marino asked.

The woman kept glaring at him, breathing in deep, raspy inhalations.

Marino said, "You're Mrs. Palmer. Betty Palmer, correct?"

Oscar crossed his arms to make an 'X' in front of his chest and said, "Wait up, wait up. Palmer? *Betty Palmer?* You're talking about... You're saying she's Ash Palmer's mom? The kid from those urban legends?" Shaking his head and walking backwards, he said, "No fucking way."

Eyes filled with tears, Regina stepped forward and asked, "Why would you do this? Wha–What did we ever do to you? We never hurt your–"

"*Quiet,*" Marino said sternly, holding a finger up to Regina's face. "I want all of you to stay back and stay quiet. I know you have questions and concerns, but this is a police matter."

"That's not fair. She killed our friends!"

"We'll get to the bottom of this, but I can't do that if you keep interfering."

"Bullshit," Regina said. "We deserve to know the truth. You don't know what we've been through, what we've seen. Kenny's dead body is on the kitchen floor right now! He's dead and she killed him! I want to know–"

"*I will* get to the bottom of this," Marino said, raising his voice but not quite yelling. "But I can't do that with an audience unless that audience stays *quiet*. If you want to keep interrupting us, I will happily take Mrs. Palmer to my car and drive her to the station where I can question her in private. Listen, I shouldn't even be talking to her right now. Not like this. I'm doing you a favor. Please step back, Ms. Park. Let me handle this."

Regina was furious. Like most of the other counselors, she wanted to attack Betty Palmer to release her anger and avenge her friends. Yet, although she disagreed with his gentle approach, she could see Marino's intentions were pure. He was in fact trying to give the counselors the closure they deserved. She walked back to Oscar's side and nodded at the cop, as if to say: '*Fine, just get it over with.*'

Marino turned his attention to Betty. He placed his hands on his knees and bent over, matching the killer's eye level. She looked angry and distant at the same time, as if ruminating about some tragic event in her life.

"What are you doing here, ma'am?" Marino asked. "Why did you attack this camp? Talk to me, Mrs. Palmer. You can make this easier for yourself."

Betty shook her head slowly.

Marino said, "You might think you're going to find some sympathy because you were shot at your age, but believe me, we will find every piece of evidence against you and haul you off to prison as soon as you get out of the hospital. Playing 'crazy' isn't going to get you out of this. But if you cooperate, I can help you–"

The front door swung open and the counselors gasped. Bishop and Miller aimed their pistols at the entrance while redeploying themselves to avoid collateral damage and crossfire.

Chelsea ran into the cabin. She fell to her knees in front of the fireplace. Her knees and hands were covered in dirt. Blood was spattered on her shirt and neck, but there were no visible injuries on her body.

Words rapidly shooting out of her mouth, Chelsea struggled to her feet and said, "The–The–They're dead. He–He killed them. He killed Jordan and

Andrea. He–He tried to–to kill me. Oh God, he's here. He's coming."

With her hands up as if she were about to lift a baby from a highchair, she walked towards Regina, then towards Oscar, then towards Marino, and then towards Betty. Despite their uniforms, it took her a moment to recognize the police. She backed up upon noticing Betty's navy coveralls.

She said, "You... You were... I just... I was running away from... from you. You killed my friends." She looked at Marino and yelled, "I swear to God, she *just* killed them!"

"It's impossible," Oscar said. "We just watched her kill... She killed Kenny, Chelsea. She's been here for, like, twenty minutes."

"No! Someone killed Jordan! He cut his head off with a machete and he–he–he threw it at me! I saw it!"

'*Machete.*' The word caused an image of Alvin's death to flash in Regina's mind. She remembered seeing a tall, burly man attack Alvin with a machete. She studied the suspect in the living room. Betty appeared to be smaller than the killer she remembered. Regina looked at Marino. She could see he was already piecing everything together.

"There's another killer," she said.

Chelsea fell to her ass and crawled back until she crashed into the fireplace screen. She tucked her knees under her chin and wrapped her arms around her shins, then rocked back and forth.

Marino said, "Miller, Bishop, there's someone else here. Backup is on the way. I want you to start securing the campsite. Make your way to the Departure Zone and through the campers' cabins." As the cops hurried out with their weapons and flashlights drawn, Marino yelled, "And don't fall for any of that bastard's tricks!"

"They had to die," Betty said in a scratchy voice.

"Excuse me?" Marino responded.

Betty ignored him. Her face strained and pale, she locked eyes with Regina. She looked as if she were about to cry.

She said, "No. They *have* to die. Your friends *have* to die. We don't have any say in the matter. We weren't given any other options. I hope you don't catch him out there. I hope he finishes the job for all of our sakes."

Regina asked, "What are you talking about? We didn't deserve any of this, you evil–"

Marino raised his hands, calling for silence with the gesture. Although they were the victims of her brutal attack, the counselors had no business interrogating the suspect. Regina clenched her jaw and breathed deeply through her nose, trying her best to contain herself. She groaned and started pacing behind the officer.

Marino asked, "What does that mean, Mrs. Palmer? Did someone force you to do this?"

"Yes," Betty responded.

"Who?"

"My son."

"Ron?"

Ron Palmer was Betty's 33-year-old son. He worked in the area beyond the forest as a farmer. Most of the locals knew him thanks to his deliveries to local grocers.

Marino asked, "Is Ron your accomplice? If he is, you need to let me know. We can bring him in *alive*, Mrs. Palmer. This doesn't have to end with more bloodshed."

"My youngest is out there, but we're not doing this because of him or me," Betty said. "We're doing this for... *Ash.*"

Marino's face twisted into a mass of wrinkles—an expression of utter bewilderment. The counselors narrowed their eyes and cocked their heads back. Their reaction said something along the lines of: '*What the fuck?!*'

Betty said, "These kids have to die, officer. They have to die in order to tame little Ash's spirit. It's part of the rules, part of the... *the agreement*. We made that agreement after Ash was killed. We upheld it in 1988 and we'll uphold it today. Thirteen counselors must die every thirteen years at Camp Blaze. If these kids are not killed, if their blood is not spilled, then Ash will rise from his grave and set the world aflame. My son must be fed in order for him to rest or... or everyone will die." Her wide, zany eyes drifted to the fireplace. She said, "Thirteen deaths every thirteen years. Thirteen deaths every thirteen years. Thirteen deaths every thirteen years."

Marino was young but experienced. He knew about Camp Blaze's history of violence. The counselors knew about it, too, but they mistook it for an urban legend.

Ash Palmer passed away in 1975 at Camp Blaze, burned at the stake like a witch by a group of deranged cultists. Only one of the cultists—Robert Lowery—was apprehended. He had referred to Ash as the 'Marked One' while confessing to the murder. He was killed after he stole a handgun from a cop's holster before the police could finish the interrogation.

Camp Blaze was shut down until 1980. In 1988, thirteen years after Ash's death, thirteen counselors were murdered at the camp. No suspects were ever identified in that massacre.

Marino asked, "Mrs. Palmer, were you responsible for the murders of 1988?" Betty smiled without emotion and nodded. Marino asked, "And Ron helped you?"

Betty nodded again.

Chelsea said, "We have to get out of here."

"We're safer here with the police than we are running around out there in the dark," Regina responded.

Betty said, "You won't be safe at all if we don't finish

the job. We're running out of time. If my count is... is correct, if Ron killed two more like she said, then we only need *two* more to end this." She looked Marino in the eye and said, "Two more dead and he'll rest for another thirteen years. Please, officer, take your gun out and shoot them. It's for the greater good."

Marino stood motionless, awed by Betty's speech. Her confession was bizarre and her request was absurd.

He asked, "Have you taken any drugs recently, ma'am?"

"Shoot them," Betty demanded.

Marino sighed, then he said, "I'm sorry it had to be this way, Mrs. Palmer." He held the radio up to his mouth, pressed the push-to-talk button, and said, "Miller, there's another sus–"

The back door swung open. Another person in hooded coveralls and an expressionless mask entered the kitchen. He held a machete in his right hand, blood smeared on the blade.

Wide-eyed, Chelsea jumped to her feet and looked over the kitchen bar. She pointed at the intruder and shouted, "It's him! Oh my God, it's him!" As she ran out through the front door, she cried, "Don't let him get me!"

Marino drew his handgun and aimed it at the killer. He kept his finger away from the trigger, though. The counselors skittered around the living room like cockroaches surprised by a bright light. Some of them followed Chelsea out the front door while others ran up to the bedrooms on the second floor. Marino didn't want to shoot through them.

The masked killer stopped near the kitchen island and glanced around. He wasn't saddened by the dead body at his feet, scared of the cop in the living room, or caught off guard by the chaos. His eyes met Betty's. He wasn't expecting to see her there. They shared a connection, communicating without making a sound.

Betty's eyes said: '*Finish the job.*'

As he made his way to the bar, pushing the scrambling counselors aside, Marino shouted, "Drop your weapon! Drop it!" The killer lunged over Kenneth's body. Marino yelled, "Don't move, Ron! Don't move!"

The killer stopped and glared at the cop.

Marino said, "I know it's you, Ron. Drop the weapon and step back or I *will* shoot. Don't make me do this."

The killer looked at Betty, then back at the cop. Tears stood in his eyes. His arms shook and his breathing grew louder.

Voice muffled by his mask, he stuttered, "I–I can't. Ash needs me."

"Ron, stop. Drop the weapon and step back."

"My brother needs me."

The killer raised the machete over his shoulder and ran forward. Marino took four quick steps back and fired three rounds at him. Two bullets entered his lower abdomen and exited through the small of his back. The third bullet shattered a rib, then came to a stop in his lung. The bullet swam in the blood flooding the punctured organ.

The killer dropped the machete, crossed his arms over his stomach, and collapsed. His upper body landed in the living room, floorboards groaning under his weight, and his legs stayed in the kitchen. Blood pooled under him as he writhed in pain.

Marino directed the panicking counselors out of the cabin. Regina refused to leave. She stood on her tiptoes and looked over the bar.

"No! God, no!" Betty shouted. She fell to her side, then crawled to the other end of the sofa. She said, "Get up, sweetheart. You have to finish this. Get up, baby, get up. You have to get up!"

The killer stopped moving. Marino kicked the machete away, then crouched next to the suspect. He rolled him onto his back and removed his mask. As expected, he found himself staring at Ron Palmer. He checked for Ron's pulse, but he couldn't find it.

As he gazed into the suspect's hollow eyes, Marino whispered, "Christ, Ron, what have you done?" He pressed the push-to-talk button on his radio and said, "Miller, get back here ASAP. We have another downed suspect. I need you to secure this damned back door. I don't want another person getting in here."

From the sofa, Betty squawked, "Ash, I'm sorry! Forgive me, baby! We failed you, son. We failed you... I'm so sorry."

Marino hurried to Betty's side. He grabbed her shoulders to restrain her. He couldn't allow her to hurt herself or anyone else. He believed she was sick, delusional and homicidal.

"You've brought death here, boy!" the woman snarled. "You've killed everyone! The world will *burn* because of *you!*"

15

MARINO HELD BETTY'S ELBOW AS HE ESCORTED HER TO the front of the camp. Regina walked behind them, arms crossed and shoulders raised. Her gaze moved between Betty and the trees. She feared there may have been another killer lurking in the woods. And, despite the handcuffs, she was afraid Betty could break free at any moment.

Regina frowned as they walked past the cafeteria. She knew Alvin's dead body was in there. She blamed herself for his death. *If I didn't stop, if I had just trusted him, he would still be alive right now,* she thought.

She whispered, "I'm sorry."

Miller stood guard in front of the cafeteria's entrance to prevent anyone from tampering with the crime scene. The cops didn't want anyone to accidentally stumble upon Alvin's dead body, either. An air of tragedy hung over the camp.

Marino looked at the group of counselors huddled together on the other side of the path. They were watching the cafeteria while discussing Miller's presence near the entrance and the murders they had witnessed and heard about. They couldn't believe the corpse of their beloved boss was inside the cafeteria.

"He's dead," Marino said as he dragged Betty past them. "There's nothing you can do to make a difference here. You might have the urge to check—to sneak around in there—but you *can't* do that. Stay out of the cafeteria. As a matter of fact, *don't move* until we tell you where to go. Got it?"

The counselors nodded at him.

As they kept walking to the front of the camp, Regina tapped Marino's shoulder and said, "They... I think I told you already, but, um... I saw one of them, one of the Palmers, attack Ricky and Maribel in the boathouse. Did you..." She paused as her throat tightened and dried. She swallowed loudly, then asked, "Are they okay?"

"They're dead," Betty answered without looking back at her.

"Quiet," Marino said, giving her arm a good tug. He pressed the push-to-talk button on the radio clinging to his chest and said, "Bishop, after you're done securing the counselors' cabin and the other suspect, I need you to check the boathouse. There may be two more victims inside. Cordon off the area when you arrive and..."

His voice became muffled as Regina stopped listening to him. She continued following him, but her mind wandered away. She thought about the Palmer family's motives. She remembered Betty's speech, but it didn't make any sense to her. She didn't believe the dead could possess the living, so there was no way Ash could have forced his relatives to attack the camp. He had been dead for decades.

She's mentally ill, Regina thought. *Or maybe she meant that she wanted to avenge Ash. Or maybe she's just a psychopath. Maybe, maybe, maybe, maybe, maybe.*

The group reached the front of the camp. Two patrol cars were parked in front of the administration building. Marino and Miller drove to the camp in one of the vehicles while the other belonged to Bishop. The cavalry was late—nowhere in sight. The driveway leading out of Camp Blaze was swallowed by the darkness.

Marino helped Betty into the back seat of his car. The woman groaned and muttered indistinctly. The pain from her injuries made her tremble. Yet, the murderous fury kept burning in her eyes.

Marino closed the door, then turned to face Regina and said, "I'm heading over to the hospital. I have some officers waiting for her there. I'd like you, Ms. Park, to travel with me."

"Why?" Regina asked in a tight voice.

"I need to take you to the precinct afterwards."

"What? No. I mean... I just want to go home. I'm tired of all of this. What else do you need from me?"

"I know this is hard for you. And it might sound like I'm just trying to make things harder, but believe me, that is not my intention. We need your assistance for this investigation. As of now, you are a... a *key* witness. Since Alvin Perry is deceased, you know the most about this camp. You witnessed the accident at the lake, Mr. Perry's murder, the incident at the boathouse, your friend's death in the counselors' cabin. We need your help to piece everything together. You can understand that, can't you?"

Regina looked back at the camp. It was dead silent. She didn't even hear the music of nature—no creaky branches, no rustling leaves, no whistling wind. Her friends grieved, but she couldn't hear them. She felt like the madness had finally ended.

"What about my friends?" she asked. "You're just going to leave them here with two cops?"

"More police, forensic specialists, paramedics, fire-fighters... *Everyone* is on their way. Your friends will get the help they need. And the campers are already on their way to a safe location. We have an auditorium ready for them in town. Their parents will pick them up in the morning. You have my word on that."

"Do you have a cell phone? I should probably call my parents if I'm going to go with you."

"I don't, sorry. But I'll make sure you can call your parents as soon as we get to the precinct. I promise."

A set of footsteps interrupted their conversation. Regina watched as Oscar approached the patrol car. He tried to smile at her, but his eyes were devoid of happiness.

He asked, "What's up? What's going on?"

Regina said, "He wants me to go with him to the police station to, um… to answer some questions."

"She's a key witness," Marino explained. "We need her for the investigation. There are some holes we have to fill and she can help us."

"Yeah, yeah, that's it. I just don't feel comfortable leaving you guys here and I don't really feel like staying awake. I just want to call my mom and go to sleep. That's all."

"Oh," Oscar said.

Marino gave him a slight nod. Oscar understood the gesture. The cop was asking for his assistance.

Oscar said, "Well, I think you should go."

Regina shook her head and said, "I really don't wanna leave you guys."

"You'd be safer at the police station. You'd be surrounded by cops, donuts, and coffee. And you can call your mom from there. Besides, it looks like everything is under control here. I can help the other cops get around the camp, too. We're fine. Yeah, everything is fine, Regina."

"You sure?"

"Positive. I'll start getting the other buses ready so

we can get the rest of the counselors out of here. Maybe I can meet you at the station later."

Marino said, "We can work something out, sure."

Oscar patted Regina's shoulder and said, "Go take care of business. Make sure these people pay for what they did to us."

Regina smiled as she knuckled the tears from her eyes. Oscar's confidence calmed her nerves. She hugged him, then they kissed.

She handed him a keyring and said, "If there are any problems, use the phone in Alvin's office to call me. And even if there are no problems, call me anyway. Talk to me. Don't... Don't forget about me."

Oscar kissed her forehead and grinned. He said, "Don't be so melodramatic. I'll see you soon, babe."

Regina walked around the car. She sat in the passenger seat. Marino closed the door for her, then he nodded at Oscar, and then he climbed into the driver's seat and got ready to depart.

As she waited, Regina stared at Betty through the rearview mirror. She felt apprehensive around the vicious killer, despite the cage partition between them, the handcuffs around Betty's wrists, and Marino's presence in the vehicle.

"You ready to go?" Marino asked.

Regina leaned on the passenger door and said, "I'm ready."

16

ANOTHER NIGHTMARE BEGINS

REGINA STARED VACANTLY AT THE WINDSWEPT TREES, watching as the branches swayed and detached leaves spiraled through the air. She saw shadowy figures dashing between the tree trunks. *It's all in my head,* she told herself. But fear poisoned her mind. She wondered if another sadistic murderer was wandering the forest. She didn't know the entire Palmer family tree after all.

What if she has another son? she thought.

The patrol car stopped at the end of the driveway. Marino looked both ways, then he took a right onto the main road.

Regina caught one final glimpse of Camp Blaze through the rearview mirror. She never imagined herself leaving the camp early. She certainly never pictured herself leaving in a police car. While looking at the rearview mirror, she noticed Betty was still rambling about the massacre.

"Thirteen deaths every thirteen years," Betty mumbled, leaning against the door. "We–We have to– to go back. We have to... We *must* kill two more before it's too late."

"Be quiet," Regina said.

Marino peeked at the rearview mirror, then watched the road ahead. He said, "Keep it down, Mrs. Palmer."

Betty's face contorted into a grimace of pain— emotional and physical. She shook her head and whimpered as she watched Regina through the rearview mirror.

She said, "I know you hate me. I don't—*can't*— blame you. But I–I only did it to save you and... and everyone like you. We *must* kill them. If we don't finish this tonight, the apocalypse will begin. The world will burn and everyone in the city—*everyone you love*—will suffer from Ash's wrath. Please believe me. I'm begging you."

Eyes wet with tears, Regina turned in her seat and scowled at the prisoner. The cage partition was the only thing stopping her from pouncing on the woman.

She said, "You killed my friends. You killed inno-cent people for no reason. Don't you understand that?"

"We–We did it for Ash. He–"

"We did *nothing* to you or your family. We weren't even born when all of... when all of *that* happened. You say there's an apocalypse coming. Well, it already arrived for us. *You* were that apocalypse. You brought nothing but pain and fear and... and sadness to my friends and our families. I can never forgive you for that. *Never*."

Regina turned in her seat and held her trembling hand over her brow like a cap's visor. Her tears plopped on her legs. She snorted with each inhale, nostrils filled with fresh mucus. Marino took a fresh handkerchief out of his pocket and handed it to her. She accepted it, looked out the window to her right, and blew her nose.

Without looking back, Regina said, "I'm sorry about what happened to Ash. I always knew the stories were more than just urban legends. I know what those monsters did to him at Camp Blaze all those years ago. I don't know how you've been able to... to keep moving after all of that. I can't imagine the pain you've endured."

Betty's thin, wrinkled lips trembled as she tried to speak, but she was speechless. She could only nod, as if saying 'thank you' and 'I'm sorry' at the same time.

Regina blew her nose again, then she sniffled and said, "But it's not right. None of this was right. What you did was... *evil*. I know your family's history at Camp Blaze, but that doesn't mean we deserved this. The victims from 1988 didn't deserve it, either. You were wrong."

Betty said, "I was right, sweetie. It was all for the

greater good. We only needed thirteen bodies—*thirteen souls*—and we would have delayed the apocalypse. But you stopped us. You've opened the door to hell. The world will burn because of you. You'll shower in your friends' blood... if it doesn't evaporate first."

"You really believe everything you're saying, don't you? You need help, ma'am. You manipulated your other son and forced him to kill. And now he's dead, too. You–"

"I did not manipulate my boy," Betty interrupted. "He understands... He understood Ash's wrath. He understood the rules. He helped me kill in '88 and he helped me again. Like I've been trying to tell you, it was for the greater good and he knew that. Thirteen dead is better than hell on earth, is it not?"

"You're sick," Regina hissed as she turned around to face the back seat. "You're a sick, disgusting bit–"

Marino coughed loudly to interrupt their argument. He had allowed them to speak in order to retrieve information from Betty without formally interrogating her. He couldn't allow Regina to descend into madness for his own selfish reasons, though.

He said, "Stop talking to her, miss. Don't let her get to you. Come on, sit forward and try to relax. We'll be at the hospital soon."

Regina turned in her seat and crossed her arms. She stared out the windshield, listening to the unintelligible chatter from Marino's radio and the purr of the engine. Betty didn't say another word. After a night of carnage, Regina welcomed the peace with open arms. She shut her eyes and, within seconds, her eyelids got heavier with the anchors of drowsiness.

Regina's eyelids fluttered as a bright light entered the vehicle through the windshield. The side of her mouth rose in a slight smile. A convoy of emergency vehicles drove past them in the oncoming lane. A patrol car led the pack, followed by an ambulance, then another police cruiser.

Marino said, "There they go. I told you everything was going to be fine." He nudged Regina with his elbow and said, "Don't worry. More police and paramedics are on their way. We should be seeing a fire truck soon, too."

Watching the vehicles speed away through the sideview mirror, Regina said, "I hope they get there soon. I wonder if the rest of the counselors will be able to go home. You think I can call them from the hospital and–"

She gasped as the ambulance exploded. The roar of the explosion echoed through the woods and the fire lit up the road like a flare. The flaming wagon flew three meters up, flipped mid-air, then landed on top of the police cruiser at the front of the convoy. The patrol car's roof immediately collapsed. The police cruiser at the back of the convoy swerved left, but the driver wasn't agile enough. They rear-ended the crushed cop car. The flames quickly spread amongst all of the vehicles. Some of the foliage next to the road was set aflame, too.

"Oh my God," Regina said.

Marino stomped on the brake pedal. The car skidded to a stop, flinging all of the passengers forward. He had witnessed the explosion through the rearview mirror. The steering wheel even vibrated when the ambulance inexplicably detonated. He checked on Betty through the cage partition. The seat belt aggravated her wounds and tightened around her neck, but she was fine.

He grabbed Regina's shoulder and asked, "Are you okay?"

"Oh my God," Regina repeated, eyes glued to the sideview mirror.

"Ms. Park! Regina! Are you okay? Are you injured?"

Regina turned to look at the officer, eyes big and fearful. Shell-shocked, she looked like she didn't recognize the cop or her environment.

"What happened?" she asked. "What the hell happened?"

"You–You look fine," Marino stuttered, struggling to stay calm. "I need you to stay here, okay? I–I have to go check on them."

"I'm coming with you."

"No. You'll wait here. I'll be right back, okay?"

"*No.* I'm not staying with her."

Marino looked at Betty, then back at Regina, then out the rear window. He didn't have time to argue or restrain the counselor. He turned on the light bar. Red and blue lights illuminated the forest, clashing with the dark orange glow of the burning vehicles. He exited the car, flashlight in hand, and ran towards the accident while reporting the sudden explosion to his dispatcher. Regina followed his lead.

Pieces of burning metal were scattered across the wide road. Shards of glass on the pavement sparkled with the flames. Sparks from the fire danced with the wind like cherry blossoms in the spring. Bloodcurdling screams escaped the crashed patrol car at the back of the convoy.

"Jesus Christ," Marino whispered as he reached the burning vehicle.

He ran back towards his car, occasionally slipping on the larger shards of broken glass. Regina stopped next to the burning cop car. The color was instantly drained from her face. Her mouth hung open, but she couldn't think of a single word to say. The awful sight stole her voice and erased her vocabulary. She crossed one arm over her abdomen and covered her mouth with her other hand as she retched.

Two police officers were trapped in the burning car. They bellowed as they tugged on their seat belts, unable to break free from their safety restraints. The skin on their faces and hands reddened and peeled while their polyester uniforms melted into their torsos.

Then their skin started to blacken and even bubble. Large blisters spread across their faces, blood gushing out of them like pus from pimples.

The men's eyes boiled, then melted like scoops of vanilla ice cream in a hot oven. The strings of goop coming out of their eye sockets blended with the blood on their peeling faces. The man in the passenger's seat fell unconscious, slumped forward against the seat belt. The driver clawed at his chest, tearing his shirt open. He tried to grab the seat belt, but he couldn't find it. Instead, he peeled strips of crisp muscle off his chest with his fingernails, leaving his ribcage exposed. His screams softened to whimpers after a few seconds.

Regina felt the heat surging from the flames. It was hotter than any campfire she had ever experienced. She stood more than three meters away from the fire, but she was already sweating.

Marino returned with a fire extinguisher from his trunk. He aimed it at the men and squeezed the trigger. The powder from the fire extinguisher failed to put out the flames. The white cloud joined the black smoke billowing from the vehicle. He shot the extinguisher at the other patrol car and ambulance. The vehicles continued burning.

He aimed it back at the burning cops. They had stopped screaming, burned to a crisp. Black flakes of their charred skin joined the sparks, smoke, and powder in the air.

Marino yelled, "Damn it! Goddamn it!"

He dropped the fire extinguisher, drew his weapon, and glanced around. He sought a perpetrator or an explanation—anything that would have helped him make sense of things. He didn't see anyone out there, though. He examined the road.

"Was there a landmine?" he whispered. He looked up at the trees and said, "No, it–it could have been a rocket. Or maybe a gas leak."

Regina stumbled onto the side of the road and vomited into a bush. Then she leaned against a tree and wept with her back to the accident. Like Marino, she struggled to find a logical explanation for the explosion. She thought: *What would a landmine be doing in the middle of the road? Why didn't it detonate when we drove past it? We're not on a battlefield, so why would anyone shoot a rocket at an ambulance out here?* None of the officer's theories made any sense to her.

Before she could start formulating her own ideas, her thoughts were interrupted by a peculiar sound. She peered into the dark trees in front of her. Her eyes widened as she heard a faint cry. It sounded like it was coming from a child—so soft yet so hurt. Then a frightening thought dawned on her: *Gators, Bears... Hawks.*

"No, no, no, no, no," she said rapidly as she pushed herself away from the tree.

"What?" Marino asked. "What's the matter now?"

"I–I didn't send them all home."

"Excuse me? Ms. Park, there was... there was just a damn explosion! We don't have time for your–"

"I forgot to evacuate some of the cabins! There are still some kids at Camp Blaze!"

"If there are children at Camp Blaze, they will be evacuated."

Regina grabbed the officer's jacket at the chest and said, "They're crying over there. Something's wrong. They're in trouble."

Marino pulled away from her grip and walked to the side of the road. His forehead crumpled upon hearing the eerie weeping.

As she teetered to his side, Regina said, "Kimberly..."

"Kimberly?" Marino repeated. "What are you talking about?"

"Kimberly is in the Hawks' cabins. I–I didn't get her out. I promised to take care of her. She's counting on me."

Marino grabbed Regina's arm and stopped her from rushing into the woods. She tried to pull away, but the cop's grip was too powerful. She glared at him. Her eyes said something like: '*Let me go.*'

"I know what you're thinking," Marino said. "But I can't let you go back there. It's too dangerous. You saw that explosion. You... You *smell* it, don't you? You smell the... the death, right? This isn't a game. I called it in already, okay? More cops are on their way here. I'll send them directly to the camp when they arrive."

"We don't have time to stand here and wait. I have to go back."

"Ms. Park, you can't–"

"I *have* to go back. I have to help Oscar and the kids. I can't leave them like this. They're my responsibility. You'd have to handcuff me to stop me. And even if you did, I'd still run to them."

Marino said, "Don't be so foolish. Palmer and her family could have planted bombs all over the road and even at your campsite. Hell, there could even be more of them out there. Her husband, her brother, her nephews and nieces... Someone might be in your camp right now and you wouldn't know what to do. Wait for a bomb squad. Wait for us."

Regina's arm slid out of his grip. She crashed into a bush and nearly lost her balance. Marino reached out to help, but she stepped away and dodged him.

She said, "No. I'm sorry, but I can't do that. I'm not under arrest. You can't stop me from helping the people I care about."

Marino sighed and glanced over at his patrol car. His options were limited. He thought about handcuffing Regina and putting her in the back of his car, but he didn't want to endanger her. He didn't have time to argue with her, either. He still had to escort Betty to the police station and update his dispatcher on the situation.

"Damn it," he muttered. "If you're going back, you have to be very careful. Find your friends, find the campers, and stick together. I'll drive Palmer straight to the station, then I'll come right back to Camp Blaze. I'll bring an army with me. I promise."

"Hurry," Regina said as she walked backwards.

She took a deep breath, then she sprinted into the woods. Marino watched her until she vanished behind some trees. He looked back at the accident and sneered, then he ran to his patrol car.

17

RETURN TO CAMP BLAZE

REGINA HURRIED THROUGH THE DARK WOODS, PLODDING across the muddy grounds, lunging over ditches, and sliding down short hills. She could hear the cries clearly now. *The campers,* she thought. Like a mother experiencing hysterical strength during an accident, she felt a burst of energy surging through her. She ran faster, bulldozing through the bushes in her path. She slowed her sprint to a jog as she passed a group of cluttered trees.

Burning leaves flew through the air. The tree branches whined as they burned. Some of the foliage and bushes were on fire, too. Regina noticed the trail of burning trees appeared to begin at Camp Blaze and end at the main road. It looked like a massive ball of fire had been thrown at the ambulance from the woods.

"Impossible," she whispered.

While crouched, she continued running through the woods. She followed the burning trees back to Camp Blaze. Over the crackling of the flames, she heard a group of girls screaming.

"No, no, no," Regina said as she emerged from the woods.

She put her hands on the back of her head and started sobbing. Her hysterical strength vanished in an instant, replaced by crippling fear.

Camp Blaze was on fire. Blankets of black smoke rose from the administration building, the recreation hall, the large pavilion, and some of the campers' cabins. The smoke swallowed the sky, the stars and moon hidden behind a massive black cloud.

Regina put a hand over her mouth and her other forearm against her sweaty forehead. She jogged through the camp, avoiding the burning buildings. She wasn't trained or equipped to stop a fire after all. She sprinted across the quad, then made her way around the cafeteria. She slid to a stop upon spotting two burnt bodies on each side of the path.

White feathers of smoke rose from the charred corpses—crisp from head to toe. Some bloody patches surrounded their blackened skin. They looked stiff, locked in the fetal position. They emitted an awful stench, too. It was a strong coppery, meaty odor. Regina's eyes watered as she dry-heaved. She looked away and hunched over, as if she were about to vomit.

"Oh God, no," she whimpered.

She took another peek at the bodies. She was hoping to identify them, worried she may have stumbled upon Oscar's burnt corpse or a pair of dead campers. They were unrecognizable due to the severity of their burns. She noticed that they were taller than her, though. She assumed they were counselors or the cops.

She said, "Oscar, no..."

She squeezed her eyes shut and ran past the bodies. Then she squinted as she felt something touching her skin, irritating her face like a swarm of pesky flies buzzing around her head. She saw black flakes flying through the air. Her eyes grew as she realized she was running through a cloud of burnt skin and clothes. She pulled her shirt up over her nose and lowered her head.

"No, no, please, no," she cried.

She sprinted down another path. Between the trees, she saw the orange glow of another fierce fire. She felt the heat from the flames filling her lungs with each panicked breath. She simultaneously smiled and sobbed upon reaching the counselors' cabin. The first floor was on fire, but she was relieved to see Oscar and Michael Baker—another senior counselor—in front of the building.

The young men were attempting to extinguish the fire from the front porch. Oscar used a foam fire extinguisher while Michael threw buckets of water at the flames. Michael had been filling the buckets at the water well pump next to the building. But their efforts were fruitless. The fire spread to the second floor, climbing up the walls and swallowing everything in its path.

"Oscar!" Regina shouted as she approached them. "Oscar, what the hell happened?!"

Oscar glanced at her upon hearing his name, then he continued spraying the flames through the doorway. The inextinguishable blaze reached the porch, causing the two counselors to back off.

"Oscar!" Regina yelled. She grabbed his wrists and shook his arms. Voice trembling with concern, she asked, "What happened?"

Oscar gazed into her eyes. Scared and confused, he looked like he was staring at a ghost. It took him a moment to really recognize her.

He said, "Regina, what... what are you doing here? How did you... Why did... Damn it, why the hell did you come back?!"

"I need your help over here," Michael said as he rushed back to the porch with two buckets of water.

Ignoring Michael, Regina said, "We could see the smoke from the road. I came back to help. But I–I can't help if you don't tell me what happened. So, *what happened,* Oscar?"

"I have no fucking idea, okay? I don't know what to tell you. The place, this camp... It just started burning out of nowhere. We were helping those two cops find their way around Camp Blaze, then we noticed the smoke around us. The buildings were on fire, Regina. I don't know how it started. It just did. We split up to try to control the fires, but they just won't go out. We spray and splash, but they *won't* go out. Then we heard a damn explosion."

Flicking tears at him with each blink, Regina pointed at herself and stammered, "I–I–I saw that explosion. It happened on the road. More cops and an ambulance were on their way here, then the ambulance just... It was, like, a... It just blew up out of nowhere. We couldn't save them. Marino is going back to the city now. He's going to get help."

Oscar sighed as he examined the burning cabin, watching as Michael hopelessly hurled water at the fire. Even with Regina's side of the story, he couldn't think of a logical explanation for the fire. They all flinched upon hearing a loud *snap* inside of the building. It sounded like the second floor was about to collapse into the first story. Oscar admitted defeat and dropped the fire extinguisher.

He looked at Regina, shook his head slowly, and asked, "Why did you have to come back? You were out, babe. You were free. You could have helped from the police station." He slid his sooty fingers across the tears on her cheeks. A single tear went down the left side of his face. With a wry smile, he asked, "Why did you come back?"

Regina said, "I couldn't leave you."

"You already lef–"

"Oscar, I... I didn't evacuate all of the cabins."

"What?" Oscar responded, head tilted and face twisted in confusion.

"I–I forgot the Hawks' cabins. I thought I got them all out, I–I really did, but I forgot the last two cabins. We were... Someone was supposed to call them. Did anyone call them?"

"I don't remember. I mean, I don't think so."

"Then the campers are still out there. We have to get them out of here before it's too late. Help me."

Oscar took a step back, closed his eyes, and pinched the bridge of his nose. He felt his stomach turning and his heart sinking. He was disgusted by his own actions. He was busy trying to extinguish a fire in an empty building while a group of young campers could have been trapped by a different blaze.

"What the hell was I thinking?" he muttered.

Regina grabbed his arms and pulled his hands away from his face. She said, "Snap out of it. I need you. Help me evacuate the rest of the camp. Please, Oscar."

"Ye–Yeah, of course," Oscar stuttered. He glanced over at Michael and said, "Mike, you need to get out of here, man. This thing isn't going out."

Michael dropped the empty buckets and groaned, exhausted but restless. He took a deep breath, but he started coughing halfway through it.

"Sh–Sh–Shit," he rasped.

"Get to Alvin's office and call 911," Oscar said as he

tossed a keyring at him. "Tell them you need the cops, the fire department, the national guard, *everyone*. And tell them to evacuate the city 'cause this fire is going to spread and it's going to spread fast. We'll go to the Hawks' cabins and get the rest of the campers."

"The city? Man, I don't think they're going to believe that. What am I supposed to tell them?"

"Just tell them the truth, Mike. We tried to stop the fire, but we couldn't. The entire camp is going to be burned to the ground in less than an hour. Maybe less than 30 minutes. And tell them about the campers. Now go. Hurry!"

As he ran off, Michael shouted, "Fine! I'll be back to help you! I'm not leaving without you!"

Oscar grabbed Regina's hand and said, "Let's get moving. We have to get them out of here before the fire spreads and blocks our exits."

The couple sprinted down the path and headed to the campers' cabins.

Regina and Oscar stopped in front of the Bears' cabins. The buildings were on fire. Although some flames had spread to the exterior, it looked like the fire had started *inside* the cabins. Black smoke exited the cabins through the broken windows. They felt a sense of relief knowing Regina had already evacuated the Bears' cabins.

Yet, Oscar couldn't help but wonder if a camper was involved in the suspected arson.

They followed the trail to the Hawks' cabins. Smoke plumed towards the cabins, but they didn't notice any fires in the area. The boys' cabin was empty, though. The door swung in the doorway. The junior counselors were nowhere in sight, either.

Oscar said, "Maybe they evacuated when they saw the smoke."

Regina pointed at the girls' cabin and said, "But look. I think they're still in there."

As they approached the cabin, they heard the girls whispering amongst themselves as well as some muffled whimpers. They were trying to stay quiet, as if they were hiding from an intruder in their home. Some of the campers peeked outside from over the windowsills.

Oscar pulled the screen door open, then tackled the front door. It didn't budge. Through the window next to the door, he could see a barricade comprised of the campers' thin mattresses. The attempted intrusion filled the girls with fear. They started sobbing and huddling at the other end of the room.

Regina knocked on the window next to the door and said, "It's okay, it's okay. Girls, it's me. It's Regina. Oscar's with me, too. We're here to help."

Oscar said, "Ladies, you did a good job blocking the door, but now I need you to move these mattresses. We have to get you out of here."

Although the interior of the cabin was dark, Regina could see the fear and reluctance on the campers' faces. All of the counselors and campers had developed a friendly bond throughout the summer. The girls' sudden distrust was worrisome. *What did they see?* Regina thought.

She knocked on the window again and said, "Please, listen to me. This is an emergency. We have to go. *Now.*"

The kids argued about the counselors, the fire, and their safety. Some of the younger campers cried loudly.

"She–She's right," Kimberly stuttered, standing behind the group. The kids kept whimpering as she made her way through them. Eyes bloodshot from all of her crying, she looked at Regina through the window and said, "She... She'd *never* lie to us."

A big, twitchy smile of pride and relief stretched across Regina's face. *Attagirl,* she thought. She was grateful to see Kimberly and the other campers alive and unharmed. The girls remained reluctant for a minute before agreeing to leave the cabin with the counselors. They worked together to remove the mattresses.

Oscar turned the knob, but it was locked. He glanced at Regina and whispered, "Did Alvin lock all of the campers in their cabins?"

"N–No, of course not."

"The door's locked, Regina. And you need a key to lock and unlock it."

"I know that already," Regina replied, raising her voice in frustration. She put her hands on the back of her head and whispered, "What the hell is going on?"

Oscar knocked on the door and said, "The door is locked. Do any of you have the key? Did a counselor give you a key or–or lock you in here? Did anyone tell you anything? Anything at all?" The girls responded by shaking their heads and whimpering. Oscar said, "Then I need you girls to try to unlock the door from your side, okay? Keep pulling and I'll keep pushing."

Holly Phelps, a twelve-year-old brunette girl, turned and pulled on the knob. Oscar pushed the door with his shoulder from the other side. He was afraid the door would burst open and hit the girl, so he showed some restraint.

"It won't open," Holly cried. She grabbed the knob with both hands and leaned back. She said, "It's... stuck."

Oscar said, "Get back. I'm going to kick it open."

He took a step back, then he kicked the door with all of his might. He kicked it two more times, then he threw his body against it, then he kicked it two more times. The wood groaned, the knob clacked, but the door remained closed.

He said, "It's not going to budge. We have to get them out some other way."

Regina clapped and yelled, "Listen up, ladies! I need you to go to the bathroom at the back of the cabin! Open the big window and I'll help you climb out! Chop-chop!" She patted Oscar's shoulder and whispered, "Keep trying."

She ran around the building. The awning windows in the main cabin were too small for most of the young campers. The frosted window in the bathroom slid open, providing the most spacious escape route.

As she slid around the corner, Regina spotted a curly-haired girl climbing out the window. It was a short two-meter drop from the windowsill to the ground. It still scared the girls, though. They had seen their peers hit their heads, break their wrists, and twist their ankles from shorter falls. Regina grabbed her waist and helped her down.

Sitting on the windowsill, Kimberly said, "I knew you wouldn't leave us."

Wrestling with an urge to cry, Regina said, "I told you: I never leave a girl behind. Besides, I never got to give you my phone number. You'll need it after this. C'mon, let's get you out of there."

Kimberly nodded. She slid off the windowsill, but she didn't take her hands off it until Regina grabbed her waist. Kimberly joined her fellow camper behind the cabin. They huddled, waiting to evacuate with the rest of their peers. A blonde girl climbed out next, followed by a redhead. *Sixteen campers left,* Regina thought.

"Holy shit!" Oscar shouted from the other side of the cabin. "Regina! Regina!"

Regina whispered, "What is he–"

She gasped and stumbled back as the window quickly slid closed on its own. The edge of the window hit a freckle-faced girl's head before she could climb through, sending her broken glasses falling to the ground outside. The window cracked upon impact. The girl's face was cut from her right temple to the corner of her eye. She fell back into the bathroom, feet sliding in the sink below her, but her left hand was caught in the window. Blood dripped from her fingers and fell from the windowsill.

"*Ow!*" the girl yelped. "Ow, ow, ow! Help! Help me! Please, please, it hurts!"

"I'm here, I'm here," Regina said as she stood on her tiptoes and tugged on the window. She clenched her jaw upon spotting the girl's swollen, bloody fingers. They were crushed so badly that splinters of broken bone came out of the knuckles at the base of her fingers. Regina said, "Just... Just close your eyes. I–I'm going to get you out of there. I just need... I have to... Why won't this goddamn thing open?!"

"Regina, please! Please, it–"

An explosion in the cabin pushed Regina and the campers to the ground. They felt the mud vibrating under their palms and feet. The flash from the blast lit up both cabins, the surrounding trees, and the horrified expressions on their faces. The *boom* from the explosion echoed through the woods along with the campers' shrieks.

Regina staggered to her feet. Through the frosted

window, she could see the campers crowding the bathroom, pushing each other in an attempt to avoid the flames in the main room. Smoke poured out through the thin gap on the window, squeezing past the girl's crushed fingers. She covered her gaping mouth with both hands. The ceaseless weeping—cries of agony and despair—broke her heart.

She slapped her hands over her ears and sobbed. She could still hear their suffering, though. And she could see their desperate, frantic movements through the window, like ants scuttling away from a child's magnifying glass in a panic.

"Help them!" Holly cried.

Kimberly pulled on the counselor's shirt and shouted, "Regina!"

Regina looked down at her, then at Holly. Their voices snapped her out of her trance. She pulled on the window, hit the glass with the bottom of her fist, and even struck it with her elbow—but to no avail. Although she could still hear some faint whimpers, she could no longer see any of the campers' silhouettes due to the black smoke in the bathroom. She could only see the freckle-faced girl's limp fingers sticking out of the window. She had suffocated due to the smoke.

"I'm so sorry," Regina said.

She stepped back and listened to the campers' throaty coughing and hoarse breaths. Two girls lay near the bathroom doorway, bodies charred by the fire.

One of those girls lost both of her legs during the unexpected explosion. After about a minute, the campers under the window started passing out one by one.

"I don't know what to do," Regina whimpered.

She wanted to continue apologizing to the trapped girls, but she knew it was a waste of time. She had to save the other campers.

She crouched in front of the traumatized survivors and said, "I want you to–to... You *need* to *run*. You understand me? You have to get away from this camp. Find somewhere to hide in the woods, get to the main road, it doesn't matter. Just run as fast and as far as possible. And stick together, okay? Go on, get out of here."

Sniffling and moaning, the girls ran into the woods. The campers held hands, helping each other walk through the rugged terrain. Kimberly stood her ground, though. She couldn't abandon her only true friend in the world.

"Kim, you have to leave," Regina said.

Teary-eyed, Kimberly said, "I can't. You promised to help me, so I'm going to help you."

"If you want to help, follow your friends to the main road and find the cops. Tell them how to get to the cabins."

"No. I'm not going anywhere without you."

"Kimberly, please!"

"No!"

Regina put her palm over her face and groaned through her gritted teeth. Kimberly's disobedience frustrated her, but she didn't hate her for it. As a matter of fact, she was impressed by the girl's bravery and determination. She was just worried about Kimberly's safety. She couldn't forgive herself if anything happened to her.

She said, "It's too dangerous, Kim. The camp is burning and people are getting seriously hurt." She pointed at the cabin next to them. She said, "You saw that. You saw what happened to your friends. I don't want that to happen to you or anyone else."

"And I don't want it to happen to you, either. I can't leave. I don't want to be alone again. Please, let me come with you. Let me protect you like you protected me."

Regina leaned to her left and looked over Kimberly's shoulder. The other survivors were gone. She was afraid Kimberly wouldn't be able to catch up to them. The woods were difficult and dangerous to navigate at night, too. And the smoke didn't help, either. She didn't have any other options.

"Don't look at the fire, don't listen to their cries. Hold my hand and do *not* let go," Regina said. Kimberly nodded and grabbed the counselor's hand. Regina said, "Oscar needs us."

"Oscar!" Regina shouted as she led Kimberly around the building. "Oscar! Where are you?!"

They turned the corner and slid to a sudden stop in front of the cabin. Kimberly cowered behind Regina. They stared at the cabin in awe. All of the windows were broken, coughing up smoke like a cigarette addict. The front door was blown off its hinges. It looked like a rocket had hit the door and detonated inside of the cabin.

Oscar lay on the ground at the bottom of the porch steps, curled into a ball. He was squirming and moaning, his clothes covered in mud. He had bloody cuts all over his arms, face, and neck. A huge clump of mud was stuck to the right side of his head, blocking his ear and muffling his hearing. Soot was powdered on the other side of his face.

The explosion threw him off the porch. Upon

landing on the ground, he sprained his ankle and cracked a rib.

Regina ran to him, then dropped to her knees and slid to his side, like a soccer player celebrating a goal. She shook him and said, "Oscar. Oscar, get up. Talk to me, babe. Say something. Are you okay? Are you hurt? Oscar, damn it, you have to talk to me."

"Ru–Ru... Run," Oscar said weakly.

"What? What happened? You have to talk to me, Oscar. Who did this? Are you injured? I can help you if you talk to me."

"Ru–Run."

"I heard you, but we have to–"

"*Run,*" Oscar growled, his spittle spraying onto Regina's face. "Run... Run from... from that."

He got onto his hands and knees, then he pointed down the path in front of the cabin. Regina and Kimberly followed his finger. Their jaws dropped.

A child walked down the center of the path. He was smaller than most of the children at Camp Blaze. He wasn't wearing any clothing. He didn't wear any skin, either. The child was *skinless* from head to toe, muscles and ligaments and tendons and veins exposed to the smoke and sparks swirling through the air. He didn't appear to feel any pain, though.

Despite his lack of skin, his boyish facial features and blank expression were visible from a mile away. His teeth and gums were visible due to his missing lips. His shiny blue eyes pierced the black smoke like headlights at night. They couldn't identify him from afar, but they knew he wasn't one of the campers. He was a supernatural being. His eyes told stories of evil and destruction.

Betty's warning came to Regina's mind: *The apocalypse*. She thought about Betty's bizarre rant. The death, the fire, the mysterious child's appearance—all of the evidence supported her prophecy.

Regina said, "That's... That's Ash."

"A–Ash?" Kimberly stuttered.

"Ash... Palmer. She was right. The apocalypse is here. How is this even possible?"

"It–It's a real monster."

As she helped Oscar to his feet, Regina said, "We have to get the hell out of here. He'll kill us if he catches us."

Oscar kept his eyes on the boy as he limped away, one arm over Regina's neck. He said, "God, look at his feet."

With each slow step, Ash left a burning footprint behind him, flames surging from the ground. He held his right hand up with his palm facing the sky. A ball of fire appeared in his hand. He swung his arm forward and threw the fireball at the survivors.

Eyes glimmering with wonder and dread, Regina, Oscar, and Kimberly gazed at the flaming ball as if they were watching a shooting star. It soared over them, sparks raining down on their heads. The fireball hit the other cabin. The front door flew off its hinges, then an explosion occurred inside the cabin.

"Go, go, go," Oscar said as he pushed Regina and Kimberly forward.

He jogged with a limp behind them, pushing through the pain. They didn't have time to sit and map out an escape route. They figured running away from the fire and avoiding Ash by any means necessary was their best option.

Regina ran with one hand on Kimberly and the other on Oscar. She shouted, "The buses are gone and the cops aren't here yet! There's nowhere for us to go, Oscar!"

"Just keep running!" Oscar yelled.

"We can't run forever! You're hurt! We need... a plan!"

Oscar pointed at the burning counselors' cabin. The building had collapsed into itself.

"We have... to get to the... cafeteria," Oscar said, out of breath.

White with fear, Kimberly glanced back at him and asked, "Why?"

As they made their way past the cabin's debris, Oscar said, "Look. It's... not on fire. And there are... weapons in there." He coughed a few times and each cough aggravated his cracked rib. Between breaths, he said, "You remember... what you did in the cabin? With the mattresses? We... We can use the cafeteria tables...

to block the doors. We can buy time there... wait for the police there."

Ash and his flames were mere specks in Kimberly's vision. The supernatural boy appeared to prefer walking to running. She believed they could outrun him, but she wasn't sure the lunch tables in the cafeteria could protect them from his explosive fireballs. At the same time, she couldn't argue with Oscar. She couldn't think of a better plan after all.

"I'll go open the doors!" Kimberly yelled as she sprinted ahead. "Take care of Oscar!"

"Kim, wait!" Regina shouted. She sighed and frowned as Kimberly continued running. She whispered, "Be careful, kid."

His arm around Regina, Oscar huffed, then he said, "Take care of *me?* Who does she think she is? Hell, I'm trying to take care of you two."

The couple shared a nervous laugh. They followed the sound of Kimberly's rapid steps, hurtling through the thick smoke and dodging the sparks from the fire. They refused to look back at their slow but dangerous pursuer.

———

Kimberly pushed the doors open. She skidded to a stop in the cafeteria and glanced around. She was saddened by its desolation—not a soul in sight. She was hoping to find the other surviving campers hiding under the lunch tables or a group of counselors regrouping in the kitchen. *At least it's not on fire,* she thought.

Kimberly held one of the doors open for Oscar and Regina. The couple hobbled through the doorway.

Regina said, "Kim, go into the kitchen and grab as many knives as you can carry. But be careful and *don't* run with them."

Kimberly ran past the food-serving counter and through a doorway to the left of the entrance. The kitchen was long and narrow. The wall under the pass-through window was lined with counters used to prepare the food. On the parallel wall, she found a large refrigerator, ovens, stoves, cupboards, and more counters.

The girl hesitated upon spotting the blood on the floor—*Alvin's blood.* Alvin's body was missing, though. She stepped around the blood and began searching for the knives.

Oscar staggered away from Regina and said, "Help her. I'll start moving the tables and blocking the doors."

"Are you kidding me?" Regina asked with a raised brow. "You're hurt. You're going to need help. We'll move the tables together."

"Stop worrying about me. Go to the kitchen and help Kim. I don't want her to hurt herself with those knives. Besides, I don't think she's ever been in the kitchen before anyway. It'll be faster if you help her."

"Oscar, I can't just–"

"The sooner you go into the kitchen and find some weapons, the sooner you can come back here and help me block the doors," Oscar interrupted.

"Why do you have to be so fuckin' stubborn?!"

A plate shattered in the kitchen.

"Regina, help her!" Oscar barked as he pushed a table towards the entrance.

Regina flinched upon hearing another dish shatter behind her. She was angered by her boyfriend's hardheadedness, but she knew he was correct. Kimberly needed her help. She groaned in frustration and ran into the kitchen. A cabinet next to a stove was open. Shards from two broken ceramic dishes were scattered on a countertop and on the floor.

The counselor noticed Alvin's blood. She closed her eyes and shuddered as she remembered the violent attack outside of the cafeteria. The sound of *clinking* silverware pried her eyes open. She saw Kimberly standing on her tiptoes near a sink, rummaging through a drawer.

"Not there, Kim," Regina said. "Over here, hurry."

She beckoned to her and rushed to a counter under the pass-through window. She opened a drawer, revealing the knife block installed inside. Knives of all shapes and sizes were stored in the knife block. She pulled ten knives out of their slits. She placed four of the knives on the counter while balancing the others in her hands, then she closed the drawer with a swing of her hips.

She nodded at the counter and said, "Grab those. Be careful, okay? We have to get back to Oscar."

"Okay."

The girl managed to hold two knives in each hand. She followed Regina back to the dining area. Oscar pushed another table towards the entrance. Regina placed her knives on the table. Then she took Kimberly's knives and put those on the table next to the others. She went to Oscar's side and helped him push the table against the doors.

Oscar sat at a lunch table and caught his breath. He smiled and nodded at Kimberly—'*Good job, kid.*' Regina approached the window next to the entrance and peeked outside. The building was surrounded by smoke.

She asked, "What's the plan? What are you going to do with all of those knives? I mean, seriously, what do you think you can do to that *thing* out there?"

Oscar said, "I really don't know. All I know is... If he comes in here, I'm going to try to stop him. And if he tries to touch you or Kim, I'm going to hurt him."

"How?"

"Jeez, Regina, I guess I'm... I'm going to throw the knives at him. If that doesn't work, then I'll get close and personal. I'll stab him."

Regina sensed the conflict in Oscar's voice. He didn't know if a blade could hurt the supernatural boy.

And, although the child was destructive and murderous, he didn't know if he could hurt a boy. He had spent so many years of his life taking care of children and building bonds with the campers that he didn't believe he was capable of harming a child.

Regina sat next to him and nuzzled his shoulder to try to comfort him. Kimberly sat next to Regina and held the counselor's hand. They looked like a young family facing certain death.

The silence in the cafeteria was eerie. The dining area was usually the loudest room when it was occupied, filled with endless chatter, laughter, singing, and gnawing and slurping. The heart-wrenching screaming and weeping outside had finally ended. All of the children trapped in the burning Hawks' cabin passed away, burned alive like Ash Palmer in 1975. The sound of crackling flames barely entered the building.

Outside, the footpaths were engulfed, buildings collapsed, and the fire spread into the forest beyond the campsite. It was hell on earth.

Oscar glared at the entrance upon hearing a set of footsteps outside. He stood up and limped over to the windows. Regina stood on her tiptoes behind him, trying to catch a glimpse from over his shoulder. Kimberly climbed onto a table towards the center of the dining area and squinted at the windows.

The footsteps grew louder with each passing second. The crackling of the flames became muffled and the whoosh of the wind vanished. They only heard Ash's slow footsteps in the room.

"It's him," Regina said, stunned.

Ash emerged from the smoke, strolling down the path next to the cafeteria. His skinless head bobbed over the windowsill with each step. His face was impossible to read, emotionless like his mother's mask. He walked past the window in front of Oscar and Regina. His footsteps stopped on the other side of the entrance.

"Find a way out," Oscar said as he grabbed the knives. He placed them on the table next to Kimberly's feet, then he grabbed Kimberly's hand and helped her down. He said, "Climb out the window in the kitchen. I'll hold him off while you two escape. Get to the main road. It's your only way out of this."

Tears raced the beads of sweat on Regina's cheek down to her jaw. Kimberly hid behind Regina, like a shy child hiding behind her mother.

Regina said, "I'm not leaving you."

"Yes, you are."

"No, I'm not."

"I'll meet you on the road later."

Regina grabbed Oscar's arm and said, "Drop this... this bullshit macho act. We don't need you to be a hero. We can leave together."

Oscar said, "He's not going to stop and you know it.

If I buy you even a minute, you two—not just you, Regina, but Kimberly, too—can escape." He leaned in closer to Regina and said, "Think about her."

Regina grimaced. *Don't say 'goodbye,'* she thought. *Don't you dare say 'goodbye' to me.* She opened her mouth to say 'I love you,' but before she could produce a sound, the doors burst open, sending the tables sliding towards the survivors. One of the doors was blown off its hinges. Burning and splintered, it landed behind the food-serving counter. The other door was barely attached to the frame.

Ash stood in the doorway, burning chips of wood flying through the air around him.

Oscar shouted, "Run!"

Speechless, Regina grabbed Kimberly's forearm and dragged her away. They stumbled across the cafeteria and slipped into the kitchen through a doorless doorway.

Oscar grabbed the largest knife—a chef's knife. He gripped the end of the handle between his thumb and index finger, as if he were handling a throwing knife. As Ash took his first step into the cafeteria, Oscar flung the knife at him. The knife spun over Ash's shoulder, barely grazing his exposed trapezius muscle.

"Shit, shit, shit," Oscar muttered.

One by one, he grabbed the knives and hurled them at the boy. One of the knives stabbed the child's chest before falling to the floor. Another blade plunged into his abdomen, so deep that only the handle stuck out of his torso. Two blades sliced his left arms. The other knives flew around Ash's body.

Fingers wrapped around his last knife, Oscar retreated into the kitchen through the doorless doorway. He crashed into a closet door. Kimberly crouched on top of a counter at the end of the kitchen, using all of her strength to try to open a jammed window. Regina stood on top of a counter next to the doorway. She held a large stockpot full of beef stew. She was unaware of Alvin's blood and skin floating in the liquid.

Oscar furrowed his brow and asked, "What the hell are you doing? I told you to get out of here! You have–"

Regina shushed him. Oscar looked at her, then at the stockpot, then at the doorway. He connected the pieces. She was waiting for the perfect opportunity to strike. She kept her eyes locked on the doorway and counted Ash's every footstep. *Come here, Ash,* she thought. *You like to play with fire? Well, let's see how you like some stew.*

As the boy stepped into the kitchen, Regina dumped the stew on Ash. White fumes spewed from the child's flesh, as if a fire were extinguished. He wobbled to his left, then to the right, disoriented like a drunk after a night of drinking. But he didn't look injured. His face remained the same—blank, motionless, *stony*.

Regina jumped off the counter and sprinted towards the window. She helped Kimberly open it, the glass rattling and wooden frame screeching. A cool breeze blew into the kitchen as the opening slowly widened.

Oscar threw a frying pan at Ash and shouted, "Hurry! I'll hold him off!"

Regina grabbed Oscar's shoulder and said, "Don't be stupid! Let's go!"

"Leave, Regina! I'll catch up with you!"

"No! We're leaving together!"

Oscar turned and pushed Regina towards the window. He said, "I can handle this. Get Kimberly out of here. Survive—for me." Regina turned into a sniveling, babbling mess, unable to form a comprehensible sentence. Oscar said, "I love you, Regina. I always loved you. Goodbye."

They kissed, then Oscar pushed her again. Tongue-tied, Regina mouthed: '*I love you.*' She wiped the tears from her eyes, then she climbed out the window. She landed on a shrub. Then she helped Kimberly escape the kitchen. Regina stared at Oscar through the open window, hoping the love of her life would change his mind and join them.

Their eyes didn't meet again.

Her cheeks as red as apples, Kimberly touched Regina's wrist and said, "We have to leave."

"Ye–Yeah," Regina stuttered. She wiped her face again, then she said, "We have to do something. C'mon, follow me."

Regina took one final glance at the kitchen. She

saw Oscar holding a knife, his back to the window. He was using himself as a human barricade—a human shield—to protect them. She didn't agree with his decision, but she respected his wishes. She led Kimberly away from the cafeteria.

In the kitchen, Oscar wagged the knife at Ash and said, "Stay back." Ash continued walking towards him, leaving a trail of burning footsteps behind him. His face tight and scared, Oscar yelled, "Stay back!"

Ash didn't stop. He moved as if on autopilot, controlled by an unquenchable thirst for blood—a ravenous hunger for charred flesh.

Oscar shouted, "I won't let you hurt them!"

He rushed forward and thrust the knife into Ash's abdomen, causing the boy to take two steps back. The blade tore into his stomach and colon. Blood spilled out of the wound and dripped onto the floor. The blood sizzled and bubbled. It looked like it was burning through the linoleum tiles. The stabbing didn't hurt Ash, though. The boy took another step forward.

Oscar twisted the knife, turning the blade in Ash's stomach. Blood spurted out of the wound. He gripped Ash's shoulder, hoping to pull him towards the blade, but his palm was immediately burned. He gasped and staggered back. The skin on his palm blistered and peeled off. He waved and blew on it, as if he had just touched a hot tray in an oven.

"What the hell are you?" Oscar asked.

Ash glared at the counselor's feet. Oscar's sneakers were set aflame. Bug-eyed, Oscar teetered back and screamed as the fire crawled up his legs. The fire quickly reached his slick hair, consuming every inch of his body. His skin blistered and bubbled, drooping like melting plastic. Then his flesh began to blacken. He crashed into a refrigerator, then he bumped into a counter.

His inner voice yelled: '*Stop, drop, and roll!*'

He was aware of the fire safety technique—he had been teaching it to campers for years—but pain and panic sent his mind into a tailspin. The human brain tended to reset during emergencies.

Oscar dropped to his knees, then he fell to his side. Most of his clothes had burned off, but some strings of his uniform melted *into* his crispy flesh. His eyeballs burst due to the heat. The red, gelatinous remains hung out of his eye sockets. His stiff limbs curled up, like a dead insect's. He looked like he could crumble into a pile of ashes with the softest touch.

Ash watched Oscar burn to death, unfazed by the violence. As soon as he was black and crispy all over, the boy walked around the burning corpse and exited the kitchen through the doorway. He left the cafeteria and, although he couldn't see the escapees, he followed Regina and Kimberly's trail. He could *feel* their presence.

REGINA AND KIMBERLY RAN TO THE SUPPLY SHED NEAR
the archery range. They had considered running to the
main road, but they weren't sure if they could outrun
Ash and they feared the police would restrain them if
they found them. Regina didn't want to get herself and
Kimberly trapped in the back of a patrol car. She was
certain the police wouldn't believe her if she told them
about Ash's supernatural presence at the camp.

'*The skinless ghost of a dead boy is burning the camp
down and killing everyone!*' The absurd explanation was
unbelievable.

Regina was determined to fight back. The police
stopped Betty and Ron Palmer with their handguns.
So, she rationalized that they needed weapons to stop
Ash. At the moment, the archery range's supply shed
served as shelter, an armory, and a war room.

As the counselor fiddled with the door's padlock, Kimberly asked, "Regina, a–are you okay?"

Regina didn't respond. Her fingers trembled on the padlock, keys jingling in her hand. She hid her face behind her disheveled hair, trying to stop Kimberly from seeing her tears.

"I'm sorry," Kimberly squeaked out. "I really liked Oscar, too. He was–"

"That's enough, Kim," Regina interrupted. "Everything is going to be okay. You just follow my lead, all right? I'll get us out of this."

Kimberly heard the grief in Regina's weak voice. She bit her bottom lip and looked down, withdrawing from the conversation. She didn't want to rub salt in her wounds. Regina blew a sigh of relief as the padlock popped open. She pulled Kimberly into the shed, then closed the door behind them. They couldn't lock it from inside, so she grabbed a chair and dragged it in front of the door.

They knew it couldn't stop Ash—nothing could stop his explosive powers—but it gave them some peace of mind.

With a tug of a beaded pull chain, a light bulb brightened the supply shed. It was a clean but dingy room. A collection of compound bows hung on the wall parallel to the shed's entrance. The arrows were neatly organized in their quivers under the bows. There was a desk to the right, the tabletop cluttered with rusty screwdrivers and broken hammers.

A black duffel bag filled with flashlights and flares was shoved under the desk. Machetes, power drills, and a fire axe hung on the wall above the table. There were two crates in the opposite corner of the room, one filled with first aid supplies and the other with water bottles and non-perishable foods.

Regina put her palms on the table and considered all of her options. *The rusty screwdriver?* A decent thrust of the blade could have been lethal against the average person. But if a knife couldn't stop Ash, then a screwdriver couldn't get the job done, either. She sneered at the hammer. *That won't hurt him*, she thought.

Her gaze drifted to the fire axe on the wall. It was love at first sight, a smirk tugging at her lips and a fire of vengeance burning in her eyes.

"The bigger, the better," she said.

She placed the axe on the table, then went over to the compound bows. She strapped a quiver to her back and grabbed a bow. As she turned towards the exit, a rusty pair of hedge shears hidden behind the crates caught her eye. A shrill *screeching* sound echoed through the archery range as she opened and closed the shears.

"You're mine," she muttered as she stared at the long blades.

Standing near the exit, Kimberly asked, "Are you going to try to kill him, too?"

The girl's soft voice startled Regina. Blinded by her

desire for vengeance, she had forgotten about the camper. She looked at her, eyes narrowed in confusion. Kimberly mistook Regina's bewilderment for anger. She shrank away from her, hands clasped over her chest. She felt like she was standing in the supply shed with a complete stranger.

"What?" Regina asked.

On the verge of tears, Kimberly asked, "Are you going to... to try to kill that boy? Are you going to fight him like Oscar did?"

Regina said, "Yeah, I'm, um... I'm going to try to stop him from hurting us. It's all we can do until the police show up." She saw some doubt lingering in Kimberly's eyes. She crouched in front of the girl and said, "I don't know if you think he's a good boy or a misunderstood kid or an angel or anything like that, but I need you to understand one thing: *He's bad*. Ash... That boy out there is evil like the rest of his family. I won't be hurting a–a child. I would never do that, but I'll do *anything* to protect us—to protect you."

"I know he's bad. That's why I don't want you to fight him. He's hurting everyone and he doesn't care. He's a real monster. He's worse than all of the monsters Kenny ever told us about at the campfires. I think he... I'm scared he's going to kill you if you get close to him. Please don't fight him, Regina."

"I have to."

"But what if he ka–kills you?"

"He won't."

"But *what if?!* Please, Regina, I don't want you to die!"

Regina felt like she was trying to swallow a hockey puck, choking on her grief and anxiety. Most children learned about the finality of death at a young age, but many didn't fully understand the concept of 'sacrifice.'

"Everything's going to be okay," Regina said.

Kimberly asked, "Do you think Oscar is okay? Do you think he's still alive? Did he stop him?"

"I–I really don't know," Regina said, her voice breaking. "But I know he did what he did because... it was the right thing to do. He did it because he cared about us, and I'll fight Ash because I care about *you*."

"If we see Ash again, does that mean–"

Regina put her index finger up to Kimberly's lips and nodded. Kimberly got the message loud and clear —'*Yes, it would mean Oscar is dead.*' Regina just couldn't say those words. She was afraid if she said it aloud that it would come true. Kimberly started crying.

Tears flowing down her own cheeks, Regina rubbed Kimberly's shoulder and said, "Kim, you're going to grow up to be a gentle, caring, beautiful young woman. You're going to go to school and you're going to make so many friends. Some of the people you meet will be bad, especially some of the boys, but I promise you'll find some *kind* and *amazing* people just like you out there." She wiped the tears off Kimberly's face with the back of her hand. The girl kept sniveling, mucus bubbling out of her nostrils. Regina said, "No matter what happens here—to Oscar, to me, to all of us—I want you to survive. I want you to live and... and be happy. You broke out of your shell this summer, kiddo, and I think the world is ready to meet you. Just be yourself and everything will be fine."

Kimberly grimaced and shook her head. She appreciated Regina's advice. It was motivational, optimistic, and sincere. But, facing a life-or-death situation, the heartfelt advice sounded more like a final goodbye.

"I'm scared," she cried. "I don't want you to die. Please, Regina, don't die."

Regina pushed the sweaty hair away from Kimberly's eyes and said, "I told you: Everything's going to be fine. Maybe... Maybe you should leave. You can still catch up to the others or get to the road. I can draw you a map or something. Yeah, we can get you out of here."

"I don't want to leave. I want to stay with you. Please don't make me leave. And don't leave me."

Regina laughed nervously, then she said, "Okay, okay. Then let's escape together."

"Re–Really?"

Regina said, "Sure. I don't think I can convince you to leave by yourself anyway. But we're not leaving without a fight. If Ash is coming for us, he'll be coming through the archery range. I need you to stay behind me and listen to *everything* I say. And if anything happens to me, I want you to promise me you'll run. Okay?" Kimberly lowered her head. Regina put her finger under her chin, lifted her head, and repeated, "*Okay?*"

Kimberly nodded reluctantly and said, "Okay."

"Thank you, sweetie. Thank you..."

The camp was shrouded in smoke. Only the dark orange glow from the burning buildings and trees pierced the black clouds. The sounds of trees collapsing, wood snapping, and flames crackling roared through the campsite. The archery range was relatively tranquil, though. The wind blew some of the smoke away from the field, leaving only some curly plumes spiraling through the air.

Regina and Kimberly crouched behind a circular foam target at the end of the shooting range. They saw Ash walking towards them on the neighboring path.

"I think I hear the cops," Kimberly said as she gazed into the woods to her right.

Without taking her eyes off Ash, Regina said, "I hear them, too. We just have to buy some time." She prodded Kimberly with her elbow, then she whispered, "Remember what I said: Stay behind me and run if anything happens."

"I will."

"Attagirl."

Ash walked onto the lawn. The blades of grass

ignited under his feet, revealing his path. Like an ant attracted to sugar, he was drawn to the survivors.

Regina emerged from behind the target with the compound bow in hand. She shouted, "Stop! Ash, stop it! I know why you're here! You don't have to do this!" Ash kept walking. Regina said, "I know all about you and your... your death. I know your mother and brother. I know your mom, damn it! Can't you understand me?! I know *Betty Palmer!*"

Ash stopped in his tracks, flames flickering out from under his skinless feet. He tilted his head to the side, as if he were trying to understand Regina's speech. His facial expression remained the same —*vacant*. The boy gazed at Regina. But in his mind's eye, he saw his mother, Betty Palmer, standing in front of the foam target.

It worked, Regina thought. *Maybe he does understand us. Maybe he's just looking for his mother.*

She said, "I know what they did to you. Those cultists... They were bad people. Evil people, Ash. But we're not like them. We're... We were innocent. Your mom, Betty Palmer, I think she can help you find your way back home. I can take you to her or–or I can bring her to you. Just don't hurt us. Please, Ash, stop this."

Ash brought his head back upright. The façade faded, the mask slipping off Regina's face. He saw the counselor and camper again.

He looked at the toolshed to his right. The shed *exploded* with his glare. Burning planks of wood flew every which way, soaring across the archery range like flaming arrows.

"Okay, Plan B," Regina whispered.

She shot an arrow at Ash. It struck the boy's chest. His sternum broke with a *crunching* snap. Geysers of blood sprayed out of his ruptured heart. He took two wobbling steps back, then he marched forward.

"Shoot him again!" Kimberly cried out from behind the target. "Hurry!"

Regina shot another arrow at Ash, missing his head by a foot. She shot a third arrow at him. It whizzed past his ear. She was panicking—palms sweating, arms trembling, legs shaking—despite the boy's slow pace. Her fourth arrow flew over his shoulder.

"Oh, fuck this," she muttered. She threw the bow at the ground, then she grabbed the fire axe in front of the foam target. She yelled, "Close your eyes, Kim!"

Kimberly squeezed her eyes shut and held her hands over her face. She wanted to cover her ears, too, but she had to keep them open to hear the outcome of the confrontation.

Regina raised the axe overhead and ran across the field. Ash continued walking, undaunted by the weapon. The counselor swung the axe at the boy's neck. The blade sank into his throat, severing his jugular and windpipe. A long spray of blood shot out of his neck. The big, heavy drops pattered on the lawn like rain. The hot blood set the grass ablaze.

Ash teetered until he stood only on his left foot.

Regina tugged on the axe's handle, but she couldn't retrieve her weapon. The blade was trapped in his neck. So, she kicked Ash's stomach. The boy lost his balance and fell to the ground. Regina felt some resistance as she stepped forward, as if her foot had sunk into a puddle of mud. She noticed the sole of her sneaker had melted.

She lunged forward and stomped on the butt of the axe head. The blade plunged deeper into his throat, piercing his esophagus and scraping his cervical vertebrae. He was halfway decapitated.

While Ash squirmed on the ground, Regina ran back to the foam target. She slid to a stop, grabbed the hedge shears, then ran back to the skinless child. Kimberly peeked out through the slits between her fingers. She saw Ash on the ground and Regina running into the flames. In her eyes, Regina resembled a superhero.

Before Ash could sit up, Regina opened the shears as wide as possible and thrust the blades into the ground *over* the boy's neck. The blades sliced into his throat above the axe head while pinning him to the ground. She closed the shears to drive the blades into Ash's neck, opened them, then closed them again.

Grunting and groaning, she repeated the process. She snipped away at his neck, cutting through the durable muscles and veins and tubes and bones. Gurgling and crunching sounds emerged from the huge hole on his neck. Flames licked up from the lawn under Ash's head, dancing around his skull. But his flesh didn't cook or burn.

Yet, even as Regina mutilated his throat, the vacant expression stayed on Ash's face. He gazed at the counselor with a set of hollow eyes.

Regina shouted, "Go to hell!"

She closed the shears and decapitated the boy. His head rolled to her left, leaving a trail of flames in its path. She released the shears, fell back on her ass, and crawled back. She stared at the body for a long moment, awed by her own actions. She felt like she had just beheaded a real child. The idea made her skin crawl.

She glanced over her shoulder and spotted Kimberly peeking out from around the foam target. Stiff and pale, the camper was obviously traumatized by the mayhem.

As she crawled towards Kimberly, Regina said, "Don't look. Please don't look." Kimberly sniffled and shut her eyes. Regina hugged her and said, "It's over. We can go home now. I promise, I'm going to take you home, Kim. It's over, sweetheart. It's finally over."

Kimberly sobbed into Regina's chest. Regina kissed the girl's head while trying to stop herself from breaking down. She glanced around the camp. A few junior counselors and campers had escaped during the chaos, but they appeared to be the only survivors at the campsite now. They were surrounded by death, breathing in the ashes of their burnt friends with each inhale.

Why couldn't I stop this? Why am I still alive? Regina thought.

She looked back at Ash, then at the burning structures throughout the camp. Although she could barely see them through the smoke, the trees around them burned, too.

She said, "We can't leave through the woods, Kim. We'll have to leave on a rowboat. You like the lake, don't you?" Kimberly nodded. Regina forced a smile and said, "Good. Let's go home."

She held her hand out, wrist up, as if to say: '*Do you still trust me?*' The violent beheading scarred Kimberly's mind, but she saw the kindness and love in Regina's eyes. She took the counselor's hand. Regina picked up the compound bow, then they started heading to the docks.

THE COMPOUND BOW ON THE FLOOR BETWEEN HER FEET, Regina helped Kimberly board a rowboat at the end of the dock. The calm water rippled under their boat as they paddled away.

"Close your eyes," Regina said.

"Why?" Kimberly asked.

"Just for a minute, Kim."

"O–Okay."

Kimberly shut her eyes while Regina kept paddling. The counselor maneuvered around the dead bodies and capsized boats floating in the water, avoiding them like naval mines. The victims—more campers than counselors—floated facedown. Some of them were unintentionally drowned by the panicking kids that couldn't swim.

As she paddled, Regina glanced over her shoulder, then at the dock at the other side of the lake. *Just get her to the other dock,* she told herself. *We'll be home free if we can just get across the lake.*

"Can I open my eyes now?" Kimberly asked.

"Give me one more minute."

"Okay. Um... Regina, can I ask you a question?"

"What is it?"

Eyes closed, Kimberly asked, "Do you think he's really dead?"

Regina leaned to her right and gazed into the dark forest beyond the lake, as if she were expecting to spot Ash waiting for them. The coast was clear.

She asked, "What are you talking about, Kim?"

"Do you think that boy, Ash, is really dead? If he's like a... a ghost or something, do you think you actually stopped him? Is he dead?"

Regina said, "Yes. I think Ash is dead. I don't know how he came back in the first place or what will happen to him, but I think he's gone for good now."

Kimberly opened her eyes. A cautious smile broke on her face. She didn't notice the dead bodies in the lake. Regina smiled back at Kimberly. She bit her fingernails, then she snickered, and then she leaned back in her seat and giggled deliriously. Her laughter echoed across the lake. Tears joined the sweat on her face. Kimberly cried, too.

As she recomposed herself, Regina said, "I have no idea how I'm going to explain this to the police. I mean, what am I supposed to say? Ash came back from the dead and burned the camp down? The boy who was killed here *decades* ago somehow returned and killed all of these innocent people? It sounds crazy to me and I saw the whole thing. God, what am I going to do? What am I going to say?"

Society held up a thin line between sanity and insanity, and Regina was forced to tightrope across that border.

How can I explain the unexplainable? she thought.

Kimberly said, "I'll tell them whatever you want me to tell them. I saw him, too. If we both have the same story, maybe they'll believe us. When me and my sister would mess something up at home, we'd blame it on something else together and our parents always went easy on us after. And maybe there are other campers and counselors out there. They could have seen him, too, right?"

Regina said, "You're a sweet girl, Kim. I appreciate the offer, but... I don't want to drag you deeper into this. Remember what I said at the archery range. I want you to live a normal life. You deserve that. If you tell them about Ash, they'd put you in a psychiatric hospital. Let me handle this, okay? If you really want to help, just follow my lead."

"Okay. Thank you, Regina."

"Thank you, too. I wouldn't have gotten this far without you. You're braver than you think. You know that, don't you? Someday, you're–"

"Regina!" Kimberly shouted as she jumped to her feet and pointed behind the counselor.

Regina turned around in her seat. Ash marched towards the end of the dock, the camp burning behind him. His head was reattached to his neck.

"The kid just won't die," Regina said as the rowboat reached the center of the lake.

She loaded the bow and aimed it at the dock. The boat's rocking didn't help her accuracy. The dock was farther than the entire length of the archery range, too. She held her breath, steadied her aim, then released the arrow.

Whoosh!

The arrow flew two meters over Ash's head and struck the dock. The skinless boy's pace didn't change. He had just been beheaded with an axe and hedge shears. Arrows couldn't scare him.

Regina shot three more arrows at him in rapid succession. Two landed in the water and one hit the dock.

"No, God, no," the counselor whispered.

Ash stopped at the end of the dock and stared at his grotesque reflection in the water. He took a step back, as if frightened by the liquid. He glanced over at Regina with his head cocked to the side. Then he glared at the water near the rowboat, setting off an underwater explosion. As if a whale had dove into the lake, a huge wave of water burst into the air.

Regina and Kimberly fell into their seats and screamed as the boat rocked violently. Hot water rained down on them, soaking their clothes and stinging their skin.

Kimberly lurched towards Regina. She took the compound bow out of her hand and yanked an arrow out of her quiver.

"Kimberly, wait!" Regina yelled.

"I can do this!"

Kimberly loaded the bow and aimed it at Ash. She felt time slowing around her as she focused on her target. She could see each droplet of water raining down on them, sparkling in the periphery of her vision. The crackling from the fire and the splashing from the water vanished in an instant. For a brief moment, the lake was dead silent. She released the arrow as she exhaled.

The projectile penetrated Ash's throat. It snapped his spine and stuck out from the back of his neck. He tottered around, his head spinning like a basketball on someone's finger. As he fell to his knees, he glared at the rowboat again.

An explosion occurred under the boat. Regina gasped and Kimberly shrieked as they were hurled four meters into the air. Kimberly landed headfirst in the water. Boiling blood squirted out of the wound on Ash's neck. A string of hot, gooey blood hung from his bottom lip. The child fell to his side, lifeless.

Regina held her breath and swung her head in every direction as she searched for Kimberly underwater. The water was darker than usual due to the blanket of smoke covering the sky. Water clogged her ears, too. She couldn't hear or see a thing. She swam to her left, then to her right, then down. Kimberly was nowhere in sight.

Close to suffocating, Regina swam up and surfaced from the water near the overturned rowboat. She spotted Ash's dead body at the end of the dock.

She yelled, "Kim! Kim, where are you?! Answer me, sweetie! Please, Kim, talk to me! Kimberly!" There was no response. She examined the water near the dock, then she glanced over at the opposite dock. She said, "No, no, no. Please let her be okay. Don't do this to us. Please, please, please."

She drew a deep breath, then she submerged her head in the water. She searched for the missing camper again. The girl was gone, though. A minute passed, then two. She popped her head out of the water and gasped for air, then she sobbed.

"Kimberly! Kimberly, please! Damn it, don't leave me like this," she cried. Once again, no one answered. Regina whispered, "I'm so sorry. I should have sent you away. It's all my fault. This is all my fault. Please... Please forgive me."

Weakened by her depression, Regina sank into the lake. She couldn't endure the emotional pain. Her head pounded and her chest ached. *She's gone,* she thought. *She's dead because of me.* She contemplated suicide—a slow, painful death to punish herself for her failures. But each time she was close to passing out, her head bobbed out of the water and she drew a deep breath.

Survival instincts were hardwired in every human's mind. A little voice inside of her told her to keep fighting. She tried to ignore it, but it just grew louder with each attempt to drown herself.

Whimpering, Regina swam away from the capsized rowboat. She headed to the other side of the lake.

WATER DRIPPING FROM HER WET HAIR AND SOPPING clothes, Regina crawled onto the shore and vomited. She grasped at vines and branches as she clambered up a hill. At the top, she got to her feet and walked unsteadily to the dock. She tried to open the shed to her right, but it was locked. She looked at the forest behind her. Exhaustion—physical and mental—talked her out of running through the woods.

She sat down and caught her breath. From her position, she could see Ash's body on the parallel dock across the lake. The boy was still incapacitated. Her eyes wandered to the water. Her mouth dried up and a lump blocked her throat. Short, raspy breaths escaped her pale lips.

"Kim–Kimberly," she stuttered, her voice barely loud enough for herself to hear it.

She crawled to the end of the dock. A girl floated

facedown near the capsized rowboat. She was a small girl, short and thin. A beam of moonlight pierced the smoke above and dawned on her body, revealing her blonde hair. And Kimberly was one of the few blonde-haired girls at the camp.

Regina's face scrunched up. She said, "It's not her. It can't be her. It's not Kim... It's not you..."

She closed her eyes to stop herself from seeing the dead bodies in the lake. But she couldn't stop the images of death from flashing in her mind. Hiero-glyphs of murder were carved into her inner eyelids. Then her nose wrinkled upon catching a whiff of the burning forest and baked human remains. She had escaped the camp and swam to safety, but she couldn't run from reality.

Rocking back and forth, she mumbled, "Why? Why? Why? Th–This can't be real. Why is this..."

Her voice faded and her eyes opened to a squint. She stood up and looked behind her, lips trembling, cheeks twitching, legs wobbling.

She heard a thrumming sound.

"Tha–That's a... a helicopter," she said. She stepped back until she reached the end of the dock, one step away from falling into the lake. She said, "It has to be real. Has to be. Has to be. Has to be..."

She kept her eyes on the sky above the trees. The thrumming grew louder. Then a white-and-blue police helicopter came out of a black cloud of smoke. It stopped over the lake. The occupants appeared to be surveying the extent of the damage while canvasing the area for survivors.

While doing jumping jacks, hopping and waving, Regina shouted, "I'm here! I'm here! Don't leave me! I'm still here!" The helicopter continued hovering without moving. Regina yelled, "Please! I'm here! I'm..."

She stopped as the helicopter turned around. The cabin door was open. She couldn't help but smile as she saw someone pointing down at her. The helicopter flew closer, then it hovered over the dock. They couldn't fly closer due to the tall trees. They couldn't land without a helipad or clear landing zone, either. A black roll-out ladder was unfurled and lowered from the helicopter's cabin. It dangled about a foot above the dock.

Regina had climbed plenty of ladders before, but she had never clambered up to a hovering helicopter. She breathed deeply to shake off her jitters, then she started climbing.

"Don't look down, don't look down, don't look down," she said as she moved up the ladder.

She felt her grip loosening because of her clammy palms. Her hair swung all over the place due to the wind from the helicopter's rotor, partially blinding her. Three rungs away from the cabin, a man reached out to her. She was relieved by the mere sight of his skin. She climbed up and grabbed his hand, then she was pulled into the cabin.

As she fell into a seat, breathless and dizzy, Regina turned to face her savior.

Officer Dominic Marino sat on the seat closest to the cabin door. Drenched in sweat, he could feel the unearthly heat from the fire in the helicopter. He rolled the ladder up while looking out at the burning campsite. He witnessed the explosion on the road, he knew something was afoot at Camp Blaze, but he wasn't expecting to find an unstoppable fire raging through the forest.

"Are you okay? You hurt?" Marino asked as he glanced at Regina.

Regina responded, "I–I'm alive."

Marino could see she had been through hell. He didn't notice any severe wounds on her body, though.

He said, "I told you I was bringing an army. The cavalry is on its way. What the hell happened down there?"

Regina pursed her lips and shook her head at him. She looked out at the camp. The forest had turned into a sea of flames. She saw the flashing emergency lights as fire trucks and ambulances raced to the camp from every angle. Then her eyes grew and her pupils expanded while the hair on the nape of her neck prickled.

Ash stood on the dock, staring up at the helicopter. He was watching the counselor from afar, persistent like a stalker.

Regina screamed at the top of her lungs and fell off

her seat. Marino caught her and stopped her from falling out of the cabin.

"What happened? Hey, what's wrong with you?" Marino asked. "Regina, stop. Ms. Park, stop it! You're going to hurt yourself!"

"He's alive! God, no, he's still alive! We have to kill him!"

"Who?! Who, Regina?!"

"Ash! Ash is on the dock! He's alive! We have to stop him! We... We have to stop the apocalypse! She was right! Ash is here! Shoot him! Kill him! Do something!"

Marino examined the lake. He was saddened by the small bodies floating in the water. He didn't see anyone on any of the docks, though.

He shook Regina's shoulders and said, "Snap out of it. There's no one there. You hear me? Ms. Park, listen to me! There is no one there!"

Regina stopped screaming as she gazed into Marino's eyes. She could tell he was telling the truth. She looked out the cabin again. She saw Ash standing at the end of the dock, staring back at her with his cold, emotionless eyes. An image of a burning city—a hellish metropolis—flashed in her mind. She saw it as a premonition. She buried her face in the officer's chest and wept.

Marino was baffled by Regina's erratic behavior. She reminded him of Betty Palmer. He checked the lake once more. The dock was still empty.

He shouted, "Get us back to the city! There's no one else here! Go!"

As the helicopter flew away from the camp, Regina shook her head and mumbled, "N–No, no. We–We can't leave. Thirteen deaths... every thirteen years. Don–Don't you get it? We have to stop him. We have to... to stop Ash from burning the world. We have to stop... *the apocalypse*. Thirteen deaths every thirteen years..."

JOIN THE MAILING LIST

Want to visit Camp Blaze? Well, when the renovations are finished, I'll let you know when the camp is reopened for business. But seriously, I hope you enjoyed this novel. Maybe someday—perhaps in thirteen years—I'll release a sequel to this book. And if you're not interested in sequels but you enjoyed this book or *parts* of it, I highly recommend you sign up for my newsletter. I regularly publish compelling, provocative extreme horror novels. Slashers, sadistic romance, brutal coming of age, international revenge thrillers, supernatural, psychological... I've explored many of horror's subgenres already and I continue to break new ground every year. Nothing is off-limits.

By signing up for my mailing list, you'll make sure you don't miss my *newest* books or any of my *huge* book sales. I usually send one email a month, but you may receive two or three during busier months—or none at all if I have nothing going on. I won't spam you with blog posts or life updates (unless there's an emergency you *need* to know about) or my political views. This newsletter is strictly about my books. It always has been. Best of all, it is *completely* free. Visit this link to sign up: http://eepurl.com/bNlıCP.

DEAR READER

I originally wrote a preface for this novel to celebrate this new edition of Camp Blaze, but I deleted it since I usually cover all of that good stuff in my letter to you at the end of *all* of my books. And here we are. Another book, another letter. It's a little different this time, though. This is actually my *second* time writing this letter, isn't it? For some of you, it'll be your second time reading it. But don't close the book just yet! I promise, there's some new information in here.

Camp Blaze was first published on February 6, 2017, so I wrote it in 2016 when I was 24 years old. Until now, it was only available as an eBook. And for years, many of you asked me to bring it to paperback. So, in early 2021, I decided to do that but not without cleaning it up first. I figured I'd give it a quick scan for any typos and make some minor changes and then top it all off with a snazzy new cover. I wanted to give you a premium product.

But to be completely honest, I just wasn't happy with the original version of Camp Blaze. Although some readers enjoyed it—hell, I know a couple of readers who would say this is their favorite book of mine—I wasn't feeling it anymore. It was my voice, still my story, but the writing wasn't very good. And you could argue that the writing isn't very good now—your opinion is *your* opinion—but trust me, this version is *much* better than the original. So, minor adjustments turned into major edits, and the major edits led to a complete overhaul.

This isn't just a re-release. I call it an 'Author's Enhanced Edition,' but it's much more than that. This is essentially a remake. I'd say I rewrote about 85% of the original content. I reworked most of the dialogue, added new scenes, and turned the brutality up a couple of notches. The book's original word count was 43,678 from front to back. This new edition comes in at about 52,000 words, *excluding* this letter and the front matter. This was a massive project for me. It was like writing a whole new book.

But the story is pretty much identical to the 2017 version. Camp Blaze was originally inspired by classic slashers. *Friday the 13th* and *Sleepaway Camp* were two of the main inspirations. I aimed to recreate that same atmosphere with this book. You'll notice that a lot of my earlier slashers were inspired by classic movies. For example, *Butcher Road* was inspired by *The Texas Chainsaw Massacre* and *The Social Media Murders* was inspired by *Scream*. At the same time, I also wanted to change things up a bit. Some people might not like the supernatural elements in this book, but it was a breath of fresh air for me—and it was a lot of fun to write!

Most of my books are grounded in reality. I love studying and exploring taboo subjects, I love *writing* about the things that are difficult to *read* about, but even I need some escapism from time to time. This project helped me escape back in 2017 and it helped me escape now.

I have no immediate plans to publish a sequel. Back in 2017, however, I did toy around with the idea of writing a prequel. It was called '*Camp Blaze 1988.*' It was going to be a similar slasher, but it wouldn't have had any of the supernatural elements found in this book. (Remember, Betty and Ron succeeded in delaying the apocalypse by killing 13 counselors in 1988, so Ash couldn't have made an appearance back then.) I still have the outline for that project. I might release it someday just for fun. But, if you'd like to see me actually write this prequel, you should make your voice heard.

So, if you enjoyed this book, *please* don't forget to leave an honest review on Amazon. Reviews on your blogs, Facebook groups, YouTube channels, Bookbub and anywhere else are also appreciated. I might not be able to respond to all of your reviews, but I see and hear you. And if you need help writing your review, try answering questions like these: *Did you enjoy the book? Was it suspenseful? Did you enjoy the death scenes?* (Don't worry, this is a work of fiction, so you won't sound like a psychopath if you answer 'yes' to that last question.) *Would you like to see more slashers from me? Would you like to see more Author's Enhanced Editions of my older digital-exclusive books?*

And, seriously, if you would like to see more Author's Enhanced Editions in the future, make sure you mention that. Drop a review and tell me which book you'd like to see receive the 'enhanced' treatment next. These books take a lot of time and money to produce. Your words—your appreciation and support—make it worthwhile.

I'm writing this letter on April 29th, 2021. It's been a very busy year for me so far. I've released three books already, I've written a couple of short stories, and I've had to deal with my taxes here in Japan *and* back in America. (Seriously, I can't believe I still had to pay taxes to the federal government and California despite living in Japan—and paying taxes here—for over 14 months now just because I'm self-employed.) And now I have to apply to renew my visa, which I can't do online for some ridiculous reason. On top of all of that, the vaccine rollout in Japan has been *painfully* slow. I'm happy for all of you who have managed to get vacci-nated, but I'm also a bit jealous. I'm sorry if these past few letters have been filled with complaints. It's been a rough time—rougher than usual. I'm still writing, though. I have a nice collection of *new* books planned for the second half of this year. I'm already planning some stuff for 2022, too.

If you'd like to read more of my books, please visit my Amazon's author page. You'll find a small library of extreme horror books waiting for you to devour. Craving another slasher? Check out my latest release, *Night of the Prowler*. It's a nasty slasher full of suspense and violence. If you thought this one was a breeze to get through, go test your limits with *Night of the Prowler*. Looking for an extreme horror novel with deep characters and compelling themes? I highly recommend my reimagining of the Kuchisake-onna/Slit-Mouthed Woman urban legend, *Am I Beautiful?* I feel like that's my most complete experience. My next book is titled *The Girl in the Attic*. I'll hopefully share more about that book in early June. It's a project I've been working on for a long time. Thank you very much for the support. Your readership, your messages, your reviews, your likes and shoutouts and all that good stuff on social media has kept me going through these hard times. I'll never forget that.

Until our next venture into the dark and disturbing,

Jon Athan

P.S. If you have any questions or comments, or if you're an aspiring author who needs *some* help, feel free to contact me directly using my business email: info@jon-athan.com. You can also contact me through Twitter @Jonny_Athan or my Facebook page or even follow me on Instagram @AuthorJonnyAthan. It might take me a while to get back to you, but I always try my best to respond. Thanks!

Printed in Great Britain
by Amazon

The Man Who
Made Plants Write